PENINSULA SINKING

PENINSULA SINKING

STORIES

DAVID HUEBERT

A JOHN METCALF BOOK

BIBLIOASIS
WINDSOR, ON

Library and Archives Canada Cataloguing in Publication

Huebert, David, author
          Peninsula sinking / David Huebert.

Short stories.
Issued in print and electronic formats.
ISBN 978-1-77196-192-9 (softcover).--ISBN 978-1-77196-193-6 (ebook)

          I. Title.

PS8615.U3P46 2017   C813'.6   C2017-901949-X
                                                                C2017-901950-3

Readied for the Press by John Metcalf
Copy Edited by Allana Amlin
Typeset by Ellie Hastings
Cover designed by Martyn Schmoll

 Canada Council **Conseil des Arts**
for the Arts **du Canada**

 ONTARIO ARTS COUNCIL
CONSEIL DES ARTS DE L'ONTARIO
an Ontario government agency
un organisme du gouvernement de l'Ontario

Canada Ontario
Ontario Media Development
Corporation

Published with the generous assistance of the Canada Council for the
Arts, which last year invested $153 million to bring the arts to Canadi-
ans throughout the country, and the financial support of the Government of Canada. Biblioasis also acknowledges the support of the Ontario
Arts Council (OAC), an agency of the Government of Ontario, which
last year funded 1,709 individual artists and 1,078 organizations in 204
communities across Ontario, for a total of $52.1 million, and the contri-
bution of the Government of Ontario through the Ontario Book Publishing Tax Credit and the Ontario Media Development Corporation.

PRINTED AND BOUND IN CANADA

 MIX
Paper from
responsible sources
FSC® C004071

for Natasha

CONTENTS

ENIGMA

Serge is asking what more can I do. He puts his hand on my shoulder and each finger is a splash of acid. I know he wants to help but I also know *what more can you do* means *your horse is on massive doses of tranks and analgesics, your horse is a giant skeleton walking, your horse is lame and life for a lame horse is no life at all.* Serge is saying all this without saying it and I am brushing his hand away and wishing I could brush away these truths that have begun to wilt me. Wishing I could simply live inside my colossal love for that animal. Serge is saying you don't have to make a decision right now and I am thinking her name over and over, thinking *Enigma Enigma Enigma.* I am thinking, as I have been for days, about what it means to founder this badly, to have to walk on bare bone. I am once again trying to imagine that animal's enormous pain, thinking if I could only conjure that feeling I could absorb a portion of her agony. Thinking how the bone that shot through her hoof after the laminitis spread is known as the "coffin bone," thinking that a horse injected with barbiturate becomes toxic shortly after death. Thinking how it's crucial not to give other animals the chance to scavenge the poisoned cadaver, thinking of the taxi driver who killed my first cat before screeching around the corner. I am thinking of the three cats I have buried in my parents' backyard and wondering once again that heinous, haunting thought: how to deal with a half-ton cadaver?

The summer after I failed math ten for the second time my parents took me and my brother whale-watching on the Digby Neck. We ate lobster rolls with lots of lobster and too much mayonnaise and cruised way out into the Bay of Fundy. We searched for two full hours and I was sure we weren't going to see anything and then the captain stood up straight and the boat gathered speed and I could see the spouts out there in the water, two miniature tornadoes shuddering through the grey-blue sky. As if the water itself had decided to dance and soar. The spouts stopped and the guide pointed to a slick black mass, rising for the surface. The whale charged straight for the boat before swerving away at the last chance and I could see its strange liquid face cresting the water. The creature became a massive, swimming grin. It was huge and dark and sublime and I heard the guide saying "humpback" and "calf" but I did not register the meaning until the mother appeared alongside, dwarfing the boat with her rubber-glove blackness. The mother left her head underwater but I felt that I knew her more than anything I had ever known. I knew the curious joy she took in the vastness of the ocean. Knew the painful lack of her lost companions. Knew her fathomless love for that grinning calf.

The mother dipped underwater and was gone, leaving a slough of foam on the surface. The calf followed shortly and the guide explained that these were humpbacks and

humpbacks were known as "clowns of the ocean" because they were so often spotted at play. Soon their twin spouts emerged a hundred metres to port and the captain turned the boat to follow and I was imagining their movements below the surface, picturing the dip and sway of tail through water, their sauntering glide through the blue-black depths. The spouts disappeared and we waited a few long minutes but the whales did not surface. I would never see these creatures again, I realized, and a bright grief bloomed in me.

As we approached East Ferry, small black dolphins began to jump beside the boat. I said to my brother I didn't know we had dolphins in Nova Scotia and my father overheard and said maybe I should take that oceanography class at school and even though I resented any school advice from my father I thought maybe I should, maybe I should.

Serge is saying maybe spend the night at home. Serge is saying *Heather it's been four days* and maybe he's right, maybe it would be good for me but there is nothing to convince me to leave this trailer at the barn with its yellowing curtains and coffee-stained fold-down linoleum table. There is nothing to convince me to leave the horse I've spent ten years of my life with, the horse I've known longer than Serge and differently. The horse that has sensed the subtleties of my body—a nervous twitch, a feint of the reins, a remote fatigue in a calf muscle. The enigma I have known in ways otherwise unknowable.

I say you're right Serge, just maybe not tonight. He holds me sweetly for a long time and I determine to let him and eventually it feels good. Serge leaves quietly and gets in his car and I watch the taillights streak along the pasture like grenadine fireflies. I walk out under the three-quarter moon, smelling the hay and grass and manure. As I enter the barn I hear her nicker, the wet shudder rising up from her tired throat. I open the stall and lie down beside her, feeding her

mints from my pocket and falling asleep, as I have for the last three nights, with my arms around the gunmetal barrel of her neck. I dream I am riding her underwater. She is part whale, now, but still somehow the same. She swims fast and sure and weightless through the endless liquid dark.

Girl goes whale-watching, is overcome by wonderment of non-human life. Girl enrolls in oceanography course at high school. Formerly troubled girl, struggling in school, whose parents felt need to repeatedly warn about sex without condoms and perils of pregnancy, realizes that taking riding lessons for entire life and nurturing deep-seated passion for animals may translate into everyday skills. Despite former mathematical ineptitude, girl takes advanced chemistry and biology and surprises parents and teachers and self with success. Girl improves high school grades, gains acceptance into university. Girl takes biological sciences at Dalhousie, works part-time cleaning stalls and shovelling manure until she makes enough money to buy a horse with help from now highly supportive parents. Writes heartfelt application essay and is accepted to Atlantic Veterinary College. Marries tall and stoic small animal vet whom she loves because of the ridiculous side of him only she knows—the way he refers to himself as "Serge the Surge," the way he cheerfully sings sordid profanities when he's frustrated by someone's driving, the way he holds the blanket in both fists and tugs it up to his chin when he's sleeping in on Saturdays, looking as adorably boyish as a square-jawed man with greying sideburns can look.

The farrier has helped me move the horse out into the middle of the back pasture, the pasture where she's often frolicked and chattered in the late evening. Serge called and said he was racing over but it is better to do it alone. Hal and Summer stand in the main pasture, not grazing but switching their tails and watching. I kneel beside her and draw a slow, deliberate

breath before slipping the needles into her jugular—a large dose of xylazine followed by the lethal barbiturate. I put the needles away and reach for the apples and mints. She casts her black eyes up and I can see that she is already sedated. I put a hand on her neck and rub as she nibbles an apple, the breath from her massive lungs slowing, slowing. Her head is in the dirt and when I lift it up I find it heavy, heavier than it has ever been before. That day we went whale-watching, the guide described how whales sleep—drifting downwards, fully unconscious, colliding softly with the ocean floor. Then rising again, still sleeping, to take air. As the final breath leaves her, I think this is how I will remember this horse: drifting and rising through an endless, liquid dream. A life without friction. Her breath is slowing, slowing, and I am digging an enormous hole in the ground, fashioning a coffin from the boards of her stall, and crawling into it with her. Wrapping my arms around her huge, heaving breast. Marvelling at the grey-white constellations of her coat. Clinging to this beloved enigma as the dirt scuffs over us.

MAXI

She stands at the morning count with her right cheekbone bulging and purpled, red lightning forked in the white of her eye. I ask how it happened and she says she fell down. "Just me or is it slippery around here," I say, looking down the line at the seven women shivering in front of house number six. "So many girls taking falls these days—do we need to put down some Krazy Glue?" I hear someone snicker and see Toothy Lucy biting back a smirk. When I ask her what's funny she shrugs, straightens up. Lucy's six one and built like a Hereford, serving life for putting a chopstick through her girlfriend's eyeball. I puff up and tell her to stop smiling, tell her I've had enough of that rotten brown picket between her lips. The smirk fades and she lowers her chin like she wants to swing. But she doesn't swing. Never has.

As I walk away Maxi gives me a look like "thank you" and I give her a glance like "don't get used to it just doing my job." I head into the house and aside from the reek of rotting fruit there's nothing amiss. On the way out I tell the girls don't think I don't know what you're doing with those Folgers tins and if I see one more hollowed-out tennis ball in the garbage can.

I buzz through the gate and squat down next to Brenda under the "No Smoking" sign behind the cafeteria. The "No Smoking" sign behind the cafeteria is where we smoke our cigarettes. Brenda, her voice rusty as the rims of her rusty Pontiac, asks how goes the battle. I tell Brenda about the shiner and she says Maxi probably deserved that one.

"It's the eyes." Brenda the diagnostician. "Seen it before. She's got that slur in her eyes."

I don't tell her what I think of Maxi's eyes—tender as crooning violins. I don't say anything, just nod and finish my cigarette and walk away wondering, not for the first time, whether Brenda has something going on with Lucy.

It was 1966 and Judy was eight years old and she'd walked out onto Truro Heights Road. Staggered up the hill into the cool night air. Staggered away from the house where her father had brought a strange woman. A woman in a red sundress with breasts pushed together, freckles dappled about like fruit flies swarming on a pair of peaches. Judy'd asked what about her mother and her father had looked straight at her and said, "What are you going to do about it?" The freckled woman clucked and leaned back on the couch and Judy fled. Fled up the hill and along the outskirts of the golf club where she stood with the oval moon coming and going as the clouds slid fast and silver. The sweet hum of fresh-cut grass and the snore of crickets ringing through the summer night. She felt herself chilly and alone in that wide empty dark and then there it was, a blue-green disk hovering a hundred metres above the golf course like some lurid cosmic marquee. Little horns here and there and a deep humming along with the clack and shutter of mechanical parts shifting. Then a set of long sharp limbs sprung out from either side, sleek and curved like the legs of a crab. Those limbs came forth swerving and neon and began to feel their way across the cricket-blaring night.

I wake up fifty-three and a half times in the night because it's deadly hot under the covers and my heart rate is up. I climb out of bed again and again to stand in front of the AC with ice and a cold towel and I find myself thinking of Maxi. Whether she might be having trouble sleeping too. I wonder if Toothy Lucy's going into her room and making her do stuff. Stuff that's hard to regulate in a progressive federal institution where women live independently in houses. Stuff that may-be some of the women want more and some want less. Stuff that maybe some of them did before they got into the facility and some of them didn't and stuff that maybe some of them learned to like.

In the morning I bring my Earl Grey up to the terrarium and pull a mouse from the canvas bag. I take the white rodent in the twelve-inch tongs and dangle it in front of Sisyphus, watch him eye it sidelong. He doesn't turn his head as I lower the mouse but he tracks its descent. He stays total-ly still, tongue prodding the air where the rodent quivers its last. Then he slinks up and hitches and darts—ninety pounds jabbing like a pool cue. Sisyphus bites and snaps that help-less rodent's neck before dragging it into his coiled length, crunching its bones while the warmth seeps away. He takes his time, drinking the blood first and then working the body into his throat where he pulps it with his jaw. I stroke him as he eats. Stroke that lovely calico skin and feel, as always, soothed by the power lurking underneath the coolness of those black and claygreen scales. The mouse is so lucky to die there, in the midst of all that power, in the steady clutch of this beautiful serpent.

It's getting close to Christmas which means tennis balls packed full of PCP flying over the walls all night and the girls fully zombified each morning. Basements lined with Folgers tins and the reek of rotten fruit climbing out of the walls and swarms of maggots under every door. The girls trying to claim they're just composting. We can try to shut it down but in a place like this you have to pick your battles. Ninety-one inmates and eleven serving life and what you want is to give some of the others a chance at recovery, not just stick them in the seg until the walls start to jabber and sing. You have to pick your battles. Which is why I don't take the pliers to Lucy's single brown tooth. Which is why I won't report her until I find a roach or a baggie in her room, why I don't send her in to have the medical team locate the contraband she's more than likely got suitcased in every available fold and cavity. Which is why I look at a girl like Maxi with sangria sloshing in her cheek and wish there was something more I could do to help her. Which is why I'd risk my job and my benefits and my bullshit life to sit with Maxi on the front porch and take a sip of that rancid basement moonshine and ask her what she'd like to do when she gets out, what meals she might miss and whether her brother will pick her up and if maybe there's a beach or a tree or a cat that makes her cry as she lies on her tough single bed and misses it.

On the way to work I crack the Buick's window and light a smoke as I drive past rows of quiet farms, the fields not yet frozen but close. A fierce wind whips through the car, carrying the ocean's chill. Half an hour in all directions and you can still taste the Atlantic from this town in the middle of the peninsula. The Mi'kmaq named this place "Wagobagitik," meaning "end of the water's flow," and now and then I think of all the flows that have ended here, all the things that have sat stagnant in this place where wind and water come to rest.

After the morning count there's a dog training session, which is where Maxi asks me why I shave my head. I'm on duty in the room where they train Shediac, the grinning German Shephard pup, to sniff for drugs. I'm thinking about who would win in a cage match between Shediac and Sisyphus when Maxi comes up and asks about the baldness.

"Why do you shave your head?"

"To keep cool."

She stares back.

"It's a condition. Anhidrosis. Got no sweat glands."

Most people I tell look sorry or ask whether I pant but Maxi looks at me soft, as if she knows me better now and she's thankful for that. I wonder would she ever but of course she wouldn't. I'm pushing sixty and she's twenty-one and it wouldn't make any sense but still I catch myself wondering.

The crab legs skittered and shuffled, that great dark beast scampering across the sky. It scuffled through the night until it was directly above her and she knew there was no point to running. She looked up and saw an opening in the front, like a large mouth, and then a long neck lashed out and bit her. A neck that twisted impossibly fast down to where she stood and clamped around her skull. Then another curled out and bit her arm, then her leg, and she felt herself rising up into that gaping black mouth, saw a fleet of tubes laid out beneath a phosphorescent glow and a glint like stainless steel. She did not get much more than a quick glance but she saw all those human faces sticking out from tubes that contained their entire bodies. She remembered her mother, then. Her pale and helpless body in the iron lung. Her mother who'd been diagnosed with polio and who would live her last eight months with her body in that negative pressure chamber, that gigantic full-body prosthetic lung. She remembered talking to her mother in that strange device and finding that she was happy to be there. Happy just to live and breathe. She'd chuckled one day and said there was no better feeling than relief. All of this in a swirl and then darkness as Judy herself entered that fleet of bright light and glinting metal.

I'm overseeing art class and Maxi is painting a landscape. Mountains and a fire-blackened forest. Woods a deep, deep green and I imagine them full of revelling witches. She's mixing green paint into black and I'm sinking into those woods, running wild with those snaggle-nosed witches, pulling a limb out of the fire and clinging fast as it blasts me up out of the canopy and across the smoke-smeared sky.

I tell myself don't do it don't do it and then I'm leaning close and whispering, "It's lovely."

"What?"

"The painting." You. You are lovely.

She looks at me, brutal and curious.

"I used to paint, you know. I did this one of Cape Split— the bluffs and the scraggly trees and the ocean. All that pristine nature and then I put a fire hydrant on top of it, at the very edge of the highest cliff."

"Oh."

"The shapes were very sort of vivid and the colours were strange. I wanted it to be like Alex Colville. Do you know Alex Colville?"

Shaking her head, Maxi rinses her brush in the plastic cafeteria water cup. I can see some people looking over and I know it's preposterous but still I whisper, "Don't mind about Lucy. She's not that tough."

A silence vast as the ring of a seashell.

"Thanks." Her face is a jungle of hurt. "But I can look after myself."

"Course you can."

I turn and lap the room, barely stable, sneaking the odd look. She doesn't pull the brush back out of its glass, just stands there following me with her eyes.

It takes a few years to learn you're not normal. First it's all breastmilk and singalongs and the unicorn rocking horse your uncle handcrafted. An infancy you remember as the taste of toast soldiers dipped in soft-boiled eggs. It takes the disruption of that lactic dreamworld to make you understand that you would come to be wretched in the eyes of others. It takes repeated warnings not to run or play too hard and then following your neighbour Cedric out into the summer sun and forty-six jubilant chaotic seconds of Coke-can soccer and then watching the skin on your shoulders and forearms wilt into a livid red rash pocked with hives. It takes your still-hale mother whisking you inside saying "Baby baby baby" and placing you between two fans while she runs a cold bath and pulls ice from the cellar. Your father creeping in to look at you in the bath and your mother shouting "Get away from her" and you would never know where that sudden rage came from.

"Didn't know you had a thing for blondes," Brenda says, lighting her rollie. I'm smoking behind the cafeteria at our 2:30 break, the laziest part of the day, and I'm peeved to be pulled from my line of thought. (Wondering if Sisyphus is hungry, wondering what he would do if I let him loose, wondering if he'd come back to me.)

"Brenda, you know I like me a nice red-headed Scottish boy with cannonballs between his thighs."

"Better be careful squeezing up next to that girl. Just saying."

I snort and take a deep draw. "Jealous?"

Brenda stands up and starts to walk away but then she stops and says, "Make sure you watch yourself. Pretty girl like that—wouldn't want to get played."

"Thanks Brenda. Glad you're looking out for me."

"Just remember what she's in here for."

I spit between my legs and scoff as Brenda walks away, but I know she's right. I know this woman with the shiny scar under her nose is right because I've told myself the same thing many times. Reminded myself that Maxi once put a knife to a woman's throat and took all the amphetamines out of a Shoppers. That she did a stint in seg after she'd padded newspapers and cotton balls under her clothes and set herself on fire. I recall that despite those gentle blue eyes there is a danger in her and I do not want to get caught in the under-tow, no matter how soft and sweet the surface looks.

Next morning there's an officers' briefing because someone's been put in the hospital. Which of course I'm gut-struck and thinking Lucy did something to Maxi and hoping it wasn't another chopstick-type event but then the warden clacks out with her insect heels and her tasteful cleavage and says that Bradley's been put in the max unit after assaulting Sheridan, who has been hospitalized due to a burn on her face. Bradley is Maxi and Sheridan is Lucy and I'm not sure, now, why I was certain this scuffle would end the other way.

After the briefing four of us light cigarettes behind the cafeteria and the new nightshift officer tells me that she was first on the scene. Apparently Lucy crept up on Maxi while she was making tea and Maxi flipped her over and stuck her head on the element, burned off an eyebrow and half an ear.

I chuckle. "Too bad she didn't knock her tooth out."

Brenda takes a long drag, stares hard into the dirt.

How does it end? A childhood without sweat glands. A child-hood where your mother is hospitalized with polio and your father is a compulsive liar running a failing tobacco shop and maxing out every new credit card he can use his wife's name to sign up for. A childhood where your mother is put into an iron lung and when you visit you can't even hold her hand. Where your only friend is a boy in a wheelchair three years younger and when he turns ten he moves to Winnipeg and gradually stops answering your letters. Where you could never join a soccer team or go to the beach and the one time you played catch with your father he threw the ball high up in the air and you raised the glove and believed you could catch it until you felt it crack into your chin, the pain somehow sharp and dull at once and your father keeling over to cackle and there could not be enough tears in your body to drown that hurt.

It ends how you might think. It ends with an apartment where you can't see the floor for all the empty Belmont cases and Deep'n Delicious cartons, dark cake clinging to plastic walls, sprouting blue beards of mould. It ends with working at a warehouse and a gas station and finally a women's prison with benefits and salary and everything else that is supposed to be but is not the answer. It ends with improv class and pottery class and painting class and jabbing a butter knife straight through the centre of each one of your Alex Colville wannabes when you finally realize that there is no class to make you less alone. It ends with a grown woman driving forty-five minutes to sit on a beach at night and look out over the ocean wondering what it would be like to sit there in the daylight and let the sun glance down as the ocean swells saline and grand. Sitting at the beach thinking about the water all around you and if only you could enter it and swim. It ends with a landfill of 6/49 tickets, the same numbers every week and the odd day of wondering whether maybe those numbers are rigged but how could you switch them after coming this far. It ends with weekends spent watching *Star Trek: The Original Series*, muting the volume so you can speak the lines to your pet boa constrictor. It ends with watching internet porn not out of desire but out of curiosity. Wanting to know what people do when they are alone in bedrooms or classrooms or sex dungeons. What people do or what they might want to do and never get a chance. Trying to feel the secret tenderness other people might feel as they watch this same video of two women ferociously unbuttoning their plaid shirts and lying down together on a bed of hay while horses whinny in the background.

I listen to the radio on the way to work and there's a story about two boys in New Brunswick who were killed by an African rock python. A calm female reporter is saying that two brothers were at a sleepover and the neighbour's forty-five-kilogram pet snake got loose, fell from the ceiling, and strangled those two little boys in their Iron Man pyjamas. I know this is a terrible tragedy but I also wonder what it would feel like to be taken into that snake's knotted clutch. Certainly, there would be desperation and terror. The snake, too, would be scared. Jailed by humans, the snake would kill from panic, not hunger. But maybe as it closed around your chest there would also be a dark rapture, a primal wonder in the encounter, an intensity of life that knows itself lost. Perhaps there would be something enormous and vital in such a death—dying wildly, flesh against flesh. Gasping breathless and the heart slowing, slowing, the snakeflesh tightening. The skitter of a tongue tasting the air, brushing an ear. Was it possible to be crushed gently, squeezed closer and closer until the self dissolved, sweet and painless, in a cold-blooded embrace?

Over the next six days I see her face only once, in the window of the max unit. She's standing on the far side of the bubble with an officer nearby as she gets served toast and tea and she looks at me through the small Plexiglas window. She looks at me and we see each other and she doesn't smile, doesn't mouth a secret code or scream "Help me." There is nothing but a long fierce look that reminds me of cheetahs prowling a zoo. Pacing up and down the length of their fence, stepping careful and taut and every muscle and ligament twitching to run.

Towards the end, Judy used to go and read to her mother in the hospital. Her mother who lay there in a fleet of white cylinders, who had become a pale head emerging from a full-body compression chamber. Her strange round coffin like some deranged NASA nightmare. Judy's mother asked her to bring books and read to her and Judy did as she was asked. She read aloud from books she did not comprehend—Walt Whitman and Sappho and the Greek myths. She did not understand those words and she feared she would never understand this yellow-eyed woman with searing red hair who had married a sailor whose very saliva seemed to be poison.

Once she had asked her mother if she was happy, there in the iron lung. Asked if she ever wanted to escape, to creep away at night. Her mother shook her head and said no, said it felt good. Said sometimes it's nice to lie immobile, sometimes it's nice to be contained. She said she had always felt she was drifting, drifting and fragile and sick. But now she was held by this iron embrace and she felt safe. Safe and, strangely, loved.

The next time I see Maxi she's on a stretcher with two paramedics walking her across the yard. She lies immobile on the board as the paramedics walk her past all the houses where the inmates stand for the 5 p.m. count. The paramedics hustling across the yard through the waning sunlight and I find myself running after them in full view of Brenda and the inmates and everyone else. I catch up, breathing heavy, and ask what happened.

"Judy," the senior paramedic says sternly.

"Please."

"If you want to help her, leave us alone."

They're getting close to the ambulance. The warden has walked out into the yard and she's wearing a crimson dress, her breasts pushed together. She and Brenda stand together watching me, their eyes full of laughter. The paramedics load Maxi into the vehicle, her face soft and still. Her face quiet as the moon and the wildness gone and I can't tell if she's alive as the paramedics clamp an oxygen mask over her mouth and close the ambulance doors.

Judy's father was killed by a suitcase when she was eighteen. He was travelling to Halifax with a woman Judy did not know and the woman had placed her suitcase on the back seat. There was construction on the highway and her father rear-ended a transport truck. It would have been a routine collision but for the suitcase, which flew straight into Charles Walsh's ginger scalp, knocking it against the steering wheel where the life seeped out of him, the woman screeching from the passenger seat as she watched the blood bubble and spurt, smelled its blunt metallic truth.

Judy learned that day that there is nothing sweeter in life than relief. That there are ecstasies great and small, self-induced and externally given, but none can rival the lovely throbbing openness that emerges after a burden has been shed. It was as if her father was a massive, rotten tongue that had been extracted from the mouth of her soul.

She smiled and laughed through the funeral, receiving grimaces from her father's co-workers and her mother's estranged sister who had travelled from Montreal. But what did she care? They weren't there when her mother was lying still and helpless in the iron lung. They weren't there when she was a little girl who had to sit at home in total shade while her neighbours made snow forts or traipsed to the beach. They would not be there years later as she spent her nights quoting *Star Trek* dialogue to her pet snake, dining on microwaved

Salisbury steak. And so she laughed, then. She laughed into the fetid air that smelled of manure and clay. Laughed so loud her voice carried across the peninsula and drifted into the Atlantic wind.

I make it through the count and stagger out behind the cafeteria. There are six or seven officers there and Brenda is telling them what happened. Telling them about the tennis ball they found in her cell. "They don't know how she got it in there, but the warden thinks it must've been an officer." Brenda looks right at me with her slithering eyes and I know. I know Brenda gave Maxi the drugs that might have killed her and I know I cannot make it through this day.

I slink across the yard and the warden is barking at me but I just mutter something about the anhidrosis and needing a doctor. I flop into the Buick and drive home, the world a warped boomerang. At home I get a wet towel and two bags of ice and sit in front of the AC for a long time but my heart won't slow down. I climb back in the Buick and drive aimless through the night and find myself at the golf course.

I rev the engine and crash through a security fence, surprised there's no alarm. No alarm so I yank the Buick left and take it down a fairway, ripping back and forth to draw tire-black serpents in the grass. I lean into the pedal and the Buick digs in and works up the hill, finally peeling onto the green, where I slash through figure eights until turf splats the windshield. When the grass is totalled I let the Buick rest and sit there listening to the grate of my breath.

There is the familiar lightness and the rash creeping beneath my shirt like a toxic caterpillar and I am looking up at the sky and waiting for it to come down and save me. Looking up at the night sky and the blackness seems to be lowering over the golf course and I am crying out into the night. Shouting "Why, why did you choose me?" and even as

I say the words I know it's because I was precious and unique. Because I was alone and desperate and I had felt the world acutely. Because these strange unseen creatures recognized an affinity in me and the only tormenting mystery is why they did not take me with them when they left.

When Judy got home the woman in the red sundress was gone and her father was on the couch with a bottle of something clear. He poured a measure into a small glass and asked if she wanted a sip. She shook her head but he placed the glass under her nose and teetered it. The liquid smelled foul and yet she took a drink and spat it straight onto the laminate floor.

Her father grinned, hoisting her up in his arms. Beamed: "My baby girl!"

She was too old for this and her father had a little trouble lifting her. Her underarms hurt. He put her down and poured himself another drink and asked where she'd gone. She said nowhere and he patted the couch beside him and said tell me. His face was gentle and she thought for a moment maybe everything could be normal. So she told him about that interstellar disk and the fleets of gleaming cylindrical beds.

Her father rose up, all the liquor and laughter drained from his face. He moved to hit her but held back. Instead, he spat on the floor of the house and called her a fool, called her a foolish little brat. Called her a disgrace and said it was all her mother's fault, said her mother had lied about the pill and he never should have married that invalid. Judy went to her room and listened to him sing to himself and shout at the television and decided she would never again tell anyone about that insectile disk in the sky.

I tell the woman at the front desk I'm Maxi's mother and she asks a few questions and waves me through. She says Maxi has had her stomach pumped and I can go see her but make sure not to wake her because she needs rest.

Brenda stands guarding the door to Maxi's room and I hear myself hissing, "You did it, didn't you?" Brenda stares through me for a fat second. Then she raises her index finger like "come here" and opens the door to Maxi's room with her other hand. Maxi's eyes flutter open and land on me. She looks lost and stoned but alive. Brenda gently takes my hand and draws me close to the bed and then guides me to sit on the edge of the mattress where she looks at me long and low. "Watch," she says, and then she stoops over Maxi and kisses her forehead and whispers "Baby" and there's a cinch in my gut as Maxi raises a delirious hand and runs one finger through Brenda's coarse greying hair. The room goes white and sour and the rash flares across my legs. I'm looking at Maxi, soft and weak and barely conscious on the bed. The wildness seeped out of her eyes and Brenda leaning over her and kissing her again and I stand up and walk to the window and beg for that crablike blue-green spaceship to appear. But there is nothing. Nothing but the thick clouds drifting silver and a hooked fang of moon.

I open Sisyphus's terrarium, take him in my arms. He climbs up my shoulder and slinks around my neck, tickling the air with his tongue. Ninety pounds of red-tailed boa sit cool and heavy on my shoulders and I feel the weight of him tighten as I settle onto my knees. I have brought him out a hundred times and how does he know that this time is different? How does he know what I want him to do?

He wends around my chest and tightens there, tightens and squeezes in intervals. As it begins I come to know what my mother meant when she whispered from the iron lung that it was nice to feel contained. Snake all around me and my lungs shrinking, tightening. Ribs cracking and something ruptures as my stomach and bowels clamp together. Human and snake, organ and flesh, Judy and Maxi, Sisyphus and the iron lung. All of it ceasing to exist in distinction and there is no more heat, no more rash, no more foul fluid or freckled cleavage or endless insatiable desire. Nothing but the coolness of scales, snakeflesh closing in. I whisper "thank you" and Sisyphus turns his head to look at me, lightning streaking through his amber eyes.

SITZPINKLER

Miles does not tell the bartender about his mother or the old Nazi. He does not mention the Botox fiasco because (a) the bartender is a stranger and (b) that was months ago now and the droopy-eyed military psychologist at Stadacona says he should be getting over it. What Miles does tell the bartender, after three double Caesars and a margarita, is that he's going back underway in two days and it's a strange thing going to bed each night fearing the same dream of sinking, lost, through amniotic dark. A strange thing to live with a species of dread that makes your brain feel waterlogged. And strange, once you're down there, to spend most of your time sitting in front of the sonar console listening up to the surface or sending out pings and thinking maybe the hatch is going to buckle and leave fifty-nine submariners scrambling for their lives. Maybe the oxygen's going to fail and everyone on board will get giddy then grumpy-delirious before realizing they're all dying of anoxia.

The bartender is a bald guy with the eyes of a wise reptile and he keeps asking more questions so Miles tells him about channel fever and his masochistic fitness-crazed XO and then gets going on psychological training. How there basically is none. How he got back from a thirty-day stint two weeks ago and now he's going down for 105 more and what they tell you during a full year of training is grit your teeth. That after your 105 you get two weeks paid leave and just focus on that when you're breathing thin air and sharing one shower and a tiny sleeping rack with fifty-eight other seamen. What they tell you is that you are special and that not many people can handle the life of a submariner, that you were made for stealth and trained for seclusion, that you are one of the Canadian military's most elite assets, an essential defender of Arctic sovereignty, and the free world will thank you for your service.

The bartender has a white guy name—Chris or Steve or Dylan or Blane. A name bland as flour. A name so normal Miles makes a mental note to not attempt to remember it while he tells Chris or Bryan or Eric or Rob about the prospect of 105 days without WiFi or any way of contacting the outside world.

The bartender asks well didn't you sign up for this and Miles says yes. Yes he signed up for this but at what point does that cease to matter? At what point are you out of options? At what point have you maxed out five credit cards and can't get another and you have no degree and your former Hitler Youth father who is twenty-five years older than your perma-tanned mother says he'll bail you out financially if you sign up for the military? At what point do you think fuck it maybe you could actually quit smoking weed and get a free education so you sign up and because you're stupid, because you miss blasting your Yamaha off kickers and buying surfboards when you feel like it, you decide to sign up for submarine duty. Sonar panel. Sign up for weeks and months under water with fifty-four men and five women and the smell of all of them festering and nothing to console you but whale songs.

"Whale songs?"

"Yeah. Mostly humpback. Humpback's the best. They're all over *YouTube*, you just—"

Miles stops then. Realizes he's being rude and makes a point of asking the bartender about himself. Asks Chris or Matt or Will or Derek whether he's upset to be working on Christmas Day and the handsome reptile just shrugs and says "time and a half." Miles finishes his watery rye and ginge and orders another and the bartender circulates, picking up glasses from tables because he's the only person working the only dingy pub in the city that's open at 10 p.m. on Christmas Day.

People continue to clack and scuff in, knocking the snow off their boots as they trudge through the door. Three ryes later a girl sits beside Miles, her hair pulled up to show a leopard-print pattern dyed into her scalp and Miles has never seen a hairstyle that so closely resembles an undergarment. He doesn't say this, though. He says "Merry Christmas" and she says she's not Christian and he says that's too bad because there are so many things he would like to confess.

He guesses gin and tonic and she lets it happen.

She says her mother's babysitting and she's already half twisted and we're all going to need sewing kits tomorrow because this is a proper tear. Before long she gets the bartender doing tequilas and whiskeys and then she's throwing salt in the eyes of a man who attempts an arm sling, tells Miles he's become a dear, dear friend.

At some point last call occurs. The bartender heads into the office and turns off the security camera and comes back out with an off-book bottle of Jameson. The strangest part of the night is not when the bartender—the place now dribbling patrons into the snow-shagged Christmas streets—leans over and hurls a thin stream of bile into the sink before turning back to the pint he was pouring, not even washing his hands.

The strangest part of the night comes later. Comes when a gregarious blind man with a bowl cut walks around handing out mushrooms and Miles takes some because all the drug testing is done and there's not much the forces can do once he's underway.

Soon afterwards Miles and the bartender and the leopard-print princess end up back at the blind man's house with the remnant stumblers. They learn that the blind man's name is Wilber and that he keeps pigeons. He's bringing pigeon carrying back. He is sending messages to pigeon keepers in Yarmouth and Fredericton and as far as Montreal. When the power goes out, he is going to be a valuable man.

"That is so North End," purrs the leopard.

By the end of the night Miles is dreamy and jagged from mushrooms and booze and he keeps checking whether there's snot on his face because everything feels leaky. He finishes Wilber's saccharine port and then circles the party for his leopard-print prowler but someone says she's already gone home with the bartender.

Miles asks Wilber whether he can see the homing pigeons so Wilber takes his arm and they walk together out into the yard. A large red shed where the birds are chirping and skittering in their separate cells, all of them wearing aluminum anklets.

When Wilber told him about the pigeons, Miles had pictured them as part of a heroic medievalish universe full of chainmail and torches and buxom sorceresses straddling taxidermied bears. But they're just pigeons, a species of bird the old Nazi calls "sky rats." Squawking and filthy and nipping each other. The floor a Pangaea of bird shit.

Miles is thinking how horrible, what a desolate life to be locked up like this and presumably carrying all the toxins and diseases a city can spew. The shrooms are peaking and everything feels slanted and awful and he is waiting for a Hitchcock hand to pull back the shower curtain.

And then Wilber walks over. Lets go of Miles' arm and approaches his pigeons, cooing, his voice a song gurgled underwater. Opens one of their cages and lets a grey and black bird crawl out onto his arm-guard. Smiles towards Miles and says, "This is Rex Murphy."

The bird's naked pink feet crawl onto Wilber's leathered forearm and he feeds it a cracker morsel from his pocket. Rex Murphy bends over to eat and Miles sees its neck, realizing for the first time that pigeons have some beautiful colouration there, a glimmer of muted fuchsia blending into green then back again. A delightful chromatic accordion wheezing through his mind. The bird pecks at the cracker and Wilber reaches out and strokes its breast and Miles thinks it might be the most intimate thing he has ever seen.

The song of the humpback whale is always a love song. Constantly evolving within the dialects of the eleven major worldwide populations, the humpbacks' undersea chorus is a perpetual conversation that qualifies as music according to all known definitions. It develops collectively and constantly, an oral tradition that has been evolving for thirty million years. Only male humpbacks sing, and their song is thought to be part of an elaborate courtship ritual, the most complex in the animal world. But even as they sing to impress or seduce females, humpbacks also sing with one another, voices crooning together as they sound their mournful dirge. The requiem rendered all the more lovely to the human ear by this lack of words—the beautiful confusion of a language beyond sense or understanding.

Miles wakes up at 2 p.m. still a little high, a fierce hangover lurking. His phone buzzing, "Dad Dad" blinking across the name display. "Dad Dad" being the name in his contacts list alongside "Jeff FlooR hockey" and "Suzy High School."

"There's my little Sitzpinkler," croons the old Nazi, his voice an oil spill. Since the age of seven or eight, Miles' father's pet name for him has been "Sitzpinkler," a German word meaning a man who sits down to pee.

"Hey Dad."

"Don't 'hey' me."

"What? Hello?"

"Merry Christmas, son."

"It's Boxing Day."

"Let's get lunch."

"Nothing's open."

"Something's open. Be there in fifteen."

Perhaps it's not fair that he thinks of his father as "the old Nazi." The man, after all, never served in the SS or any other military force. He was actually born in a suburb of Frankfurt in 1944, the son of an Austrian heiress and a prominent newspaper editor who was once photographed shaking hands with Joseph Goebbels. What is disturbing, for Miles, is that his father has never spoken about the war, that septic wound in the family psyche. The old man has never offered a hint about what his father may or may not have done to protect his family or the nation. And so the facts Miles knows are few. He knows that as a small child Rolf often ate potatoes that looked as if they had insect legs growing out of them. He knows that Rolf watched his mother die refusing food during the savage winter of 1948. The rations reduced and his mother's creamy skin turning pale, rising into harried continents of rash. His mother scrambling to the toilet to relieve her diarrhea, delirious from thirst but still refusing to eat, insisting that they give all the food to the boy. Afterwards, at his father's insistence, the boy began learning

English and French and practising the violin five hours a day. Miles knows that some years later Rolf got his Ph.D. at the Max Plank Institute and headed overseas to research plankton reproductive cellular anatomy at Dalhousie. That he has spent his life publishing and conferencing and teaching frantically, almost vicious in his belief that hard work is the only cure for life's nameless, gnawing litany of symptoms.

Rolf is among the smartest, most accomplished people Miles has ever met and so what frustrates him is that the old man will never change. Himself a permanent resident, he will continue to call people he doesn't know "immigrants" or "foreigners" based solely on appearance. When Miles mentions his old friend Dan, his father will continue to say, "Ah yes Daniel, the Jew." In spite of Facebook wars with near strangers and persistent pleas from his son, Rolf will maintain that women simply can't do hard science and that Merkel's immigration policy has caused an upswing in crime. All of this torments Miles not just because his father is a self-righteous bigot but because he knows that here is a man who has never really listened, never simply submitted, never just rested for a moment to ponder the shape of a leaf or a cloud, never given himself over to love.

The old Nazi picks him up in the new Mercedes and Miles is thinking when did Mercedes start making hideous SUVs but of course he doesn't say this. He looks out the window at the new shipyard and the harbour water beyond and asks his dad how his research is coming. His father grunts, then puts in a piece of Nicorette and chews it fast. Rolf has been chewing Nicorette since he quit smoking thirty years ago. He always chews it furiously, as if by working his jaw hungrily enough he might transform that scrub of minty alkaloid back into the rich lungful of smoke and tar he's been craving for decades.

At the Italian restaurant on Spring Garden—walls a pornography of Siciliana—it's difficult to hear each other speak. Difficult to converse with the clamour of waiters and plates and men with gleaming shirt collars ordering wines from regions they can't pronounce.

Miles broaches retirement and the old man—almost eighty now—grumbles about the pissant dean trying to force him out and then bites into a fresh white rectangle. The waiter brings their plates and Rolf balls his Nicorette and sticks it at the perimeter of his rigatoni. After a few bites, Rolf says into his plate, "So you're going under tomorrow?" Miles says yes and his father gives him a little grunt that Miles generously interprets as "Good for you." Joining the military being the first thing Miles ever did that his father did not openly criticize. Silence being, apparently, the closest he can come to praise without melting into a steaming puddle of liquefied Saxon pride.

"A hundred and five days," Miles says.

Forking, chewing. No verbal response.

Risking everything: "I'll miss you."

Rolf's eyes leap up and ask whether they just heard what they think they just heard. Miles does not deny it. Rolf glances around the dining room to see who might be listening.

They finish their meal, conversation withering like a deked kiss.

The waiter clears their lunch dishes and Rolf orders two espressos without making eye contact, which is when Miles turns a little reckless. Decides to ask about his mother. Because when you have a parent who has recently passed away sometimes all you really want is to sit and talk about it with the other parent. So while they sit there staring into tiny espresso cups he thinks might as well. Going under tomorrow and he doesn't want to be lying in his bunk thinking why didn't he so he makes an attempt.

"So."

"Yes?" Rolf upends his espresso, dabs the crème from his moustache.

"Well—"

His father's eyebrows become a jagged question mark.

"It's just a bit strange that you haven't said anything about Mum yet."

An exhale. Then, surely, revelation.

"What would you like me to say?"

"Anything, basically."

Rolf considers this. Exhales operatically. "The whole thing is just ludicrous. Humiliating. I mean—" Rolf can barely bring himself to utter: "Botox." As if that was everything that could ever need to be said. As if in no universe would he ever have to address the possibility of his son's hurt or acknowledge that he had once loved this woman.

Miles waves for the cheque, feels himself already descending into the great dark world below.

Miles sits in front of the sonar console with twenty-five seamen in the control room and Lieutenant Panchaud announcing: "Descending now, descending now." His eyes on the depth meter and his hydrophone swirling as he listens for anything unusual, hearing only the drone of propellers as Panchaud calls out ten metres, twenty, finally sixty below. On the radar there are fishing boats and freighters and container ships to watch for, even the odd mine left over from World War II.

The HMCS *Atlantis* is Victoria-class and looks basically how you imagine a submarine: a giant black tampon wearing an adorable top hat. The *Atlantis* is a diesel-electric Cold War relic built by the Royal Navy and, now that Canada has abandoned nuclear submarines, consigned to spend its dotage patrolling the colonies with the odd detour to Asia.

As the *Atlantis* begins its long northward cruise at sixty metres below, Miles' body twitches a little. The world above goes distant, vague. An embrace forgotten in the murk of dream. Tiny spasms in his quads and calves and he remembers this sensation from his last mission. Remembers his body always readying itself to bolt. Muscles twitching and flaring, but there is nowhere to go. Not even a treadmill and no matter how many push-ups or crunches you do there is no getting rid of the jolts.

So Miles imagines the water all around him. Pictures the endless dark blanket unfurling over underwater mountain ranges and gaping abysses. Miles thinks about the course the *Atlantis* will take—past the shelf break and straight over the great skid of the Laurentian Cove, keeping north of the Sohm as they turn to skirt the Grand Banks, passing just east of the Milne Seamount, then drifting over the Flemish cap and onwards into the North Atlantic Mid-Ocean Canyon, their corridor to the Arctic. The contours of the ocean floor begin to mould his mind and he feels himself a blind man seeing clouds for the first time.

"Heard about your mother," Panchaud says. Lieutenant Panchaud is acting XO, a steel-bellied man of about forty who is generally either doing crunches in the torpedo room or standing over panels in the control room, burrowing his pinky into his ear.

"Aye-aye, sir." Miles has the headphones on, listening for abnormalities and hoping for biologics.

"Botox?" Panchaud says, driving his pinky deeper.

Miles admits yeah, Botox.

The XO laughs and Miles feels a blob of salty pain form on the roof of his mouth.

"Too bad," Panchaud says, putting his ear-filthed hand on Miles' shoulder. "I heard she was a fucking rocket."

Miles sighs into his panel and knows it's a mistake.

"Seaman!?"

"Aye-aye, sir."

"You are addressing a superior officer."

Miles rises from his chair to stand at attention. Pictures his mother's body stiff and bloated, sinking through the sea. "Aye-aye, sir."

"As you were." Panchaud turns and walks away with a smirk in his step.

On his first break, Miles lies on the rack craving fresh air and staring at his toes where the little one squishes into its neighbour. They've basically become one toe and Miles spends an alarming amount of time lathering that gnarled two-headed gorgon with tea tree oil, which is supposed to keep the foot fungus from spreading. The ritual keeps him sane, or soothed. He likes the mild sting in his red, chapped crevices, the burn of menthol lilting into lung. Miles likes to think that his toes are trying to grow into one because of evolution. The same reason he only had one wisdom tooth. Humans don't need wisdom teeth anymore and we spend all our time walking in shoes so we don't need pinky toes either. Miles considers himself a man of the future, like Kevin Costner in *Waterworld*.

Although he never voiced his opinion after his mother and the rest of the adult world claimed that it was one of the worst films in cinematic history, Miles has always privately cherished *Waterworld*. Remembers eating Skittles and needing to go to the bathroom but being unable because he was mesmerized by Kevin Costner's acrobatic skipperage aboard his modified catamaran. Miles was enthralled by the Smokers with their motorized derring-do, by Dennis Hopper's gas-guzzling piratical mania, by the giant mutant fish spawned by chemicals or nuclear testing. It was 1995 and this was the first time, as far as he could remember, that Miles had seriously imagined the future of molten ice caps. But what he loved most was the idea of a man's neck opening into gills. A gilled man swimming deep under water, finding a human city. A city submerged, abandoned to the gnaw of salt and water and time. No windows or walls, just the gridded frames of algae-frilled buildings. How Miles longed then, to become like the Mariner. To grow gills of his own. To swim unencumbered towards the bottom of the sea.

Ten days underway and Miles is taking his first shower when Panchaud thumps in, stomach swelling from a recent blitz of crunches. This is bad because Miles is not showering in the shower, which is tiny and fiercely contested and next to the toilets with their reek of sepsis and sanitizer. Instead, Miles is showering in the engine room. Showering with the drain hose from the emergency drinking water tank, which is nicely warm because the diesel is running. Miles is certainly not the only seaman who showers here on occasion, but still it's not good to get caught.

"Seaman!" Panchaud roars over the echo of the diesel.

"Aye-aye, sir!" Miles barks back, dropping the hose to stand at attention. Standing wet and naked in front of a fully dressed officer. Crossing his hands in front of his genitals.

"Do you realize you are currently bathing with the HMCS *Atlantis'* reserve drinking water rations and that in time of extremity these reserve supplies could save the life of every seaman on board yourself included?"

"Aye-aye sir!" Stretching to turn off the faucet while trying to remain as close to attention as possible.

"Then why have you chosen to breach protocol and use emergency military water supply for personal bathing?"

The water cooling on his naked body. "Warm water, sir, and cleanliness."

"Do you realize you are a total and complete prima donna?"

"Aye-aye sir!"

"That you're lucky I don't have you court marshalled?"

"Aye-aye sir!"

"That you're lucky I don't make you walk naked out into the mess hall and show everyone your shrivelled little sea cucumber?"

"Aye-aye sir!"

Panchaud looks down at Miles' feet. Stares for a long time at the red and white marble of fungus and the two gnarly toes gooing together. "*Merde*," he mutters, leaving Miles naked with the diesel roaring off the engine room walls. "*Taber* fucking *nacle*."

On a submarine there is no privacy, which means no sex. At least no detectable sex. Not even solo. One shower for fifty-nine people and time in there is strictly regulated and Miles always feels like there might be someone listening. Someone sensing a change in the rhythm of the water splashing against the drain. There's talk of homosexual encounters and there are plenty of military sexual assaults but aside from a few guys flipping through porn mags Miles has never seen much evidence of desire.

Mostly he sees deflation. Libidos sublimated into endless crunches, twisted into the mirror-bright polish of the control room floor. Men sagging like the string they tie between racks. String that starts taut at the surface and gradually slackens as the *Atlantis* travels deeper and deeper. A hundred metres, two hundred, three. Mostly Miles sees submariners growing paler and paler until he's sure he can see down through them. Sure that if they took their shirts off he would see their stuttering hearts.

Submarines are one of the few places left with no WiFi, which is both nice and not nice. It's not nice because it means he can't contact anyone up top. Not his street hockey buddies or his surfing buddies or the old Nazi. It's nice because it means Miles spends most of his free time below with books. But he only has room for one or two so he spends most of his free time on this voyage reading about whale song. Often he begins by reading and ends up just lying there, thinking. Thinking about the whales riding curious in the baffles of the *Atlantis*, calling and calling and wondering why this strange creature with the boxy dorsal won't answer. Or thinking about people. Thinking about his dad, picturing the old Nazi sitting in his office wearing jackboots and chewing Nicorette while he watches weird retro porn. Thinking about his mother, about Botox.

Miles wakes in a state of bleary relief when Douglass comes in and shakes him. With his push-broom moustache and pathological knowledge of *Doctor Who*, Douglass is his closest friend on the boat. Closest friend on the boat not signifying much because Miles likes to maintain an emotional distance.

But he's always happy when Douglass tugs him out of sleep because it means biologics. So he staggers up, patting the walls and floors until he finds his uniform. Tripping into his pants as he rushes to catch Douglass on his way up the ladder to the control room.

Douglass sits down in front of the sonar panel where he's working the balls to four. An avuncular smile as he hands Miles the headset.

First a light, high chirping. A skitter fading into warble. Then a tingle and behind it a crooning like a massive, warped bassoon. Long and sweet and low. Curving beyond ends and origins, moving and moving, onward and back, a ribboning nocturne. The trace of sparklers on the retina as their glow vanishes into dark.

"Do you hear it?" Douglass says after a deep swing of bass.

Miles nods. "Humpback for sure."

"It's a chorus. Three or four of them doing the same song for the last ninety minutes, overlapping."

Miles says there's one prominent male.

"Should we say hello?"

Sometimes submarines send out a ping to whales, and sperms have been known to respond. Miles shakes his head, says they should leave him be. Should do their job and listen.

"What do you think he's saying?"

Miles shrugs, turns his mind back to the wide, warbling croon.

At the Fleet School in Esquimalt, submariners learn a lot about marine life. They learn how to differentiate the sounds of humpbacks and orcas and pilot whales from the rattle of ships and the purr of potentially hostile submarines. They learn that the American military once affixed cameras to pilot whales and trained them to track Soviet submarine activity. And they learn about whale song. About the syntax of it, the hierarchy of sounds, the variation of themes far more complex than bird song. The eleven populations of humpbacks worldwide each have their own distinct dialect, but they draw from one another—a clear example of cultural transmission. Some researchers say that because whales can sonically send and receive twenty times as much information as humans, they rival or better us in intelligence. But Miles doesn't like to think like that, to measure human against cetacean. Miles prefers to think that whales don't differentiate between song and language, don't distinguish between sense and sound. That for them meaning and beauty are one and the same.

"I think he's lonely," Douglass says. "He's lonely and he's looking for a mate. Looking for connection."

"Of course he is," Miles says. Says it and means it and bends his mind into the hydrophone, listening to that massive creature warbling out his spectacular solitude. "I hear you," Miles whispers, not much caring whether Douglass catches it. "I hear you."

What mostly happens on ship is nothing. What mostly happens is fifty-four men and five women in identical blue shirts sucking each other's precious oxygen. What mostly happens is a boredom so colossal that cleaning the ship every seven days feels like a festival. What mostly happens is thin air and seamen on their off time playing poker and watching Kurt Russell movies over and over and trying not to think about the panel catching fire or the doors bursting in. Trying not to think about the man who died ten years ago after an electrical fire aboard the HMCS *Chicoutimi* or the fact that eight years later the HMCS *Corner Brook* struck bottom during training exercises off Vancouver Island. Trying not to think about the K-141 *Kursk*, the Russian sub that sank in 2000 with 118 hands. Putin and the navy claiming it was a collision but there was no collision. The sub went down on a routine weapon test. The seamen loading dummy torpedoes for testing and one of them went off. An explosion equivalent to a hundred kilos of TNT, rupturing the hull and collapsing three of the sub's compartments. Four point two on the Richter and picked up on seismographs from Paris to Alaska. Ninety-five men dying instantly but it's not the dead who compel Miles' imagination. It is the twenty-three who survived. The twenty-three men plunging under the waist-high water to save themselves from burning to death. Staying under and staying under but finally needing to come up to breathe. Finding not air but fire and smoke. The boat filling and filling then sinking, drifting through its lethargic last descent before finally settling on the shelf of the Barents Sea.

What mostly happens on ship is brooding along at sixty metres below, rotating the sonar ears and listening for the purr of hostile submarines. Miles spends his hours fighting fatigue and listening for hostiles and watching the sonograph sketch its jagged landscapes, the range circles opening like perfect round mouths before disappearing, green ghosts rising in their wake.

What sometimes happens is snorting. What happens every twenty-four hours is rising up to periscope depth so the ship, pseudo-whale that it is, can take oxygen. Coming up to periscope depth and all the seamen feeling the elation of it, their bodies becoming one in this massive high-tensile lung as it inhales the air that sustains them. What happens once a week on calm seas is coming up into the middle of the wide blue so that a few men at a time can stagger out into the open air. Men in dry suits opening the hatch and crawling out into the sunlight or the fierce slapping chill, feeling like insects skittering about a husk of driftwood. Grinning and sun-dazed as the swells rise and splash against the slick curvature of the vessel. Not saying anything but all of them feeling the vulnerability. The precariousness of standing in a place where an unruly wave might snatch them and the smallest collision could send them sliding into a frigid indifference of black.

Afterwards, sitting around the panel extra tired from the exposure to wind and sun, from the shock of standing out there in the full oxygen and feeling the depletion, now, more than ever. Wanting to rest the eyes just a little while staring at the control room's blinking red and yellow lights. Drinking coffee until the urine comes out thick and yellow and often.

What happens just once, ten days into this fifteen-week training mission, is testing the torpedoes. Miles and everyone else in the control room prepared to die at any moment as the men in the torpedo room load the bomb. All of them studied the *Kursk* case in training and what else is there to think of now? Something in the dark depths of the mind twitching to run, something primitive unable to compute the fact that there is nowhere to go. Eyes keen on the monitors and men chewing their knuckles and waiting. Waiting dreadful as the captain checks in with the master-at-arms, who says the missile is loaded. Picturing that twenty-foot-long half-ton warhead sitting in its torpedo tube and then the captain gives the order to fire and it's probably nerves but Miles gets a feeling like the whole boat is rocking, gasping.

What happens in one brief and terrible moment is blasting a missile that cost the Canadian military one million dollars into the hull of a decommissioned American freighter. Watching on screen as the torpedo approaches.

"Two seconds to contact."

"One second."

Heat smears across the radar. Heat billows and dissipates. All the submariners cheering and high fiving as the ship buckles. That rusted ocean-going city bending and opening at the flank. The ship listing, listing sidelong. Slowly taking in water and beginning to descend.

A cheer as the captain announces: "Target neutralized." The ridiculousness of neutralizing a target with no crew or weapons but all the submariners nonetheless rapt as they watch the blips move lower. Checking the screens and Panchaud calling out numbers as the freighter fully submerges, enters the world below. Almost an hour before it finally settles on the floor of the Mid-Ocean Canyon.

A triumph. A million dollars spent to make sure our subs could take out a warship if needed and now this fractured hulk of iron sits at the bottom of the Atlantic, its side shredded open like a nightmare mouth. Off-duty seamen already hitting the rack or turning on *Total Recall* again and Miles finds himself thinking of what might grow in that hulking wreckage. Thinking about whales. How when they die their massive bodies turn to ecosystems, what scientists call a "whale fall." Those enormous bodies becoming habitats where isopods, sea cucumbers, hagfish, and lobsters sustain themselves for decades.

Miles and Douglass sit in the torpedo room drinking cheap scotch from a six-ounce plastic vial, Miles wondering why

Douglass would risk a court martial for a whiskey this coarse. Nonetheless he drinks and enjoys the sear of the awful blended whiskey and the quick buzz it gives in the thin air. When you're underway there's technically no booze but there is also, quite regularly, booze. So they drink from a plastic vial staring at the warheads in their aluminum cases and Douglass asks Miles what he does up top, for fun. Miles considers a lie about fly fishing but instead he tells the truth: surf at Lawrencetown four times a year, a floor hockey league, occasional Tinder dates, a lot of reading.

As if he hadn't heard right: "Reading?"

"Yeah."

"Like fiction?"

"Not so much. A lot of ecological stuff. Suzuki. E.O. Wilson. Naomi Klein."

Douglass says "oh" and looks at Miles like "are you hatching to snip some wires in the diesel room?" So Miles does not tell Douglass that if he could do things over, do things without several years of ski bumming then beach bumming, without multiple false starts at university and a stupidity of debt, he'd become a conservation biologist. Give less of a fuck about the shadow of his father and travel out on a sailboat studying the effects of river pollution on migration patterns.

Douglass keeps staring awkwardly into his little vial of whiskey so Miles does not mention that he thinks a lot about megastorms and rising sea levels and massive-scale extinction but he finds that a bit morbid so he also tries to think about life. The new life that might bloom in a warming world. Miles does not say how he once read that millions of years ago there were palm trees on Antarctica, how he often imagines palm trees at the bottom of the Marianas Trench. Palm trees with faces. Neon palm trees smiling to each other. Smiling and swaying in the tickle of the gulf stream, totally safe from the storms raging on the surface.

"Did you ever hear about the *Barracuda*?" Douglass asks and even though he has heard about it Miles shakes his head. Shakes his head because he's happy to sit there and listen to Douglass talk about the secret American nuclear sub that went AWOL in the eighties. The nuclear sub with a shark's mouth painted on the bow that has been spotted by divers and pilot whale cameras and shows up on someone's radar every couple of years only to disappear on the next pulse of microwaves. Some people say that the Soviets captured it in eighty-eight and have been keeping the men hostage for three decades, allowing them to surface every few months for fuel and supplies. Others say the vessel just keeps travelling on its own accord, that it got caught in a strange magnetic current and keeps circulating, now, long after all the men have withered into skeletons. An iron sepulchre drifting with the earth's steady swirl.

"You know what I think?" Douglass says. "I think something else is driving it. Something we haven't seen before. Something super-intelligent living way down in the midnight zone. Something very smart and very patient. Something biding its time."

Miles smiles, takes another corrosive swill. "Sounds like a bad episode of *Doctor Who*," he says, thinking that in fact Douglass' hypothesis might be the loveliest thing he's ever heard.

Panchaud shakes Miles awake and tells him to come down to the mess. Panchaud's got Douglass and Bull and George out in the hall already and they walk stooped and sheepish, trading glances. Three quarters of the ship snuggled into the dining quarters and the captain notably absent. Everyone gathered around Burgess who sashays tenderly as he lathers his bloated bare gut with margarine. Hair sprouting from his nipples like furry black teardrops and a pentagram of Cool Whip zazzed across his chest. The crew hooting and whistling and Miles realizing far too late that this is the Polar Ceremony. That he and the three other new seamen are entering the Arctic Circle for the first time which means getting Polarized and no way out.

First: buckets of ice. Everyone hooting and wooing and Panchaud shouting that there is a treat at the bottom of the bucket but they have to fish it out with their mouths and the last one gets the "*Surprise Polaire.*"

So Miles, Douglass, Bull, and George on all fours digging their heads into half-melted buckets of ice. Miles' scalp and ears singing frigid in the wash and Miles feels like screaming. Feels like howling out that he is a thirty-year-old man not a high-school freshman in *Dazed and Confused* but instead he sees suddenly how a person accepts something this inane. Accepts it simply because they want to not make it worse.

Miles' teeth clamp a sardine and he rises up from his bucket amidst cheers and back pats, sees that Douglass is the only seaman with his face still submerged. Sees Panchaud grab Douglass' collar and haul him up, a sneer in his eyes.

Panchaud tells Douglass to get on all fours and he does. Everyone crowded in the mess starting to chant as Panchaud climbs onto Douglass' back, one hand raised to swing a virtual lasso. Burgess lies down on his back, garishly stroking his stomach as Panchaud rides Douglass about the hall. Everyone shouting "Lick! Lick! Lick!" and "*Surprise Polaire!*" so Douglass bends and tongues the whipped cream off Burgess' swarthy breast, his push-broom moustache turning into a cloud of lather. Panchaud grinning darkly and shaking his steed. Leaning over and hissing audibly into Douglass' ear: "Every last drop."

What kind of mother dies of a Botox overdose? What kind of mother self-injects that toxin not realizing a vial of the stuff would poison the drinking water of a large city?

A vain mother, of course. A vain and tender mother. A frail, beautiful creature whose real hair colour had always been a mystery. A mother who once had too many extra dry martinis and confessed that she fell down the stairs when she was pregnant and had always suspected that was why Miles developed his deformed grappling-hook molar. A mother with eyes like watermelons. Green eyes with a mist of orange or pink and the closer you looked the more they deepened, the more they almost seemed to purr. A mother who wore cocktail dresses displaying an embarrassment of cleavage. A mother who caused him to wonder whether they'd be friends if they weren't family but whose whispered adorations—"my angel, my darling, my baby boy"—had made him feel as if there was something warm and lovely leaking all the way through him. A mother who had come into his bedroom at night when he'd grown suddenly scared of nuclear war and told him that she was weaving a force field around him. Had put up her palms as if holding curry combs and acted it out, brushing gentle ovals into the air. A mother who had moulded a force field that looked just like one of the suspended animation pods from *Alien*. A mother who had told him that every time he was scared he could reactivate that force field, a ritual he would play out until he was far too old to be scared of the dark. And even today, even that very night on the rack, he had retreated into the darkest cavern of his mind and voicelessly whispered, "Activate."

Miles can't sleep from a cramp in his calf so he drops off the rack and walks the hall. Stalks the hall barefoot until the muscles in his legs begin to loosen and the blood hums through him. Walks off the very possibility of sleep and decides to head into the control room in search of biologics. Does not expect to see Panchaud crouched over the radar. Panchaud alone on the balls to four which means he must have come

three contacts and the captain appears, buttoning his shirt, and begins to call out orders. "Set speed for twenty knots, adjust depth to thirty metres." The navigator calls out the bearings—"two, four, zero"—and the vessel turns, gathers speed.

Whispers all around and everyone looking at their screens. What begins to congeal is a picture of two ships on the surface. Ships that have not been reported and aren't responding to radio and that's all they can say.

The captain paces from panel to panel, Panchaud close behind. The captain asks for weather recon and Panchaud reports fifteen-foot swells and the captain keeps trying for radio contact. The blips on the sonar screen are increasing speed but the *Atlantis* is catching them, gliding smoothly under the alternating chop and ice.

The captain gets on the intercom and orders the master-at-arms to load torpedoes. Panchaud reporting twenty-foot swells at the surface and the blips still gaining speed. The blips seem to be fleeing, which may or may not be a good sign, and Miles finds himself squeezing the side of his panel, waiting to face all the things that are threatening to go wrong.

What becomes of a body that's been poisoned by Botox? It looks much like a body that's drowned, a body somewhat bloated, frozen into utter stillness, the nerves completely useless. It looks particularly like a drowned body if you imagine it, as Miles always does, floating downwards through the sea. Often, he thinks of his mother as she was—laughing in large Gucci sunglasses, keeping her mouth still because she was worried about wrinkle lines. And later because her mouth and cheeks were chemically frozen. Miles often thinks of her as she was but sometimes he thinks of her another way—sees her as a rigid body drifting through the ocean. Sunlight columning down and a school of mackerel glimmering past. Her arms straight at her side and her face a rigid belligerence.

At first Miles found the vision horrific, but gradually he has begun to realize that there is something peaceful about it. Something soothing about the thought of his mother drifting down into the swaying below.

The surface blips are moving faster and faster along the radar. Blips travelling at eighteen knots through the building storm and gathering velocity but the submerged *Atlantis* is faster. Then, inexplicably, they come to a stop. All three blips slow and stop and the *Atlantis* cuts speed, comes up to periscope depth.

The captain over the radio: "This is the HMCS *Atlantis* contacting unidentified vessel in Canadian waters. Please identify." Static. A typhoon of static. "Unidentified, this is Captain Jack Bernard, Commanding Officer of the Royal Canadian naval craft HMCS *Atlantis*, commanding you to identify. Over."

Below, the torpedoes are loaded into their tubes. The master-at-arms has his key inserted, ready to twist.

Then a voice. Hoarse and harried over howling winds: "Captain Bernard this is Captain Morley Savage of the SSS *Cousteau*. We've got our propellers tangled with a hostile Icelandic whaling vessel poaching Canadian waters over."

A collective gasp. Oxygen seems to pour into the control room and a few of the seamen snicker. The captain radios the Icelandic boat and uses his military officialese to tell it to smarten up. It smartens up. Lines are cut. A large minke whale—the sub-surface blip—is set free, a harpoon wedged above its left flipper. The *Cousteau* and the *Atlantis* escort the Icelandic vessel through the swells of a building storm.

Once the whaler has reached international waters, the *Atlantis* slows and watches her until it's clear she's not doubling back. The *Cousteau* says thank you and heads back into the Arctic, en route to the North Pacific. The *Atlantis* sits at periscope

depth, gathering air, and then dives back down to eighty metres below. Miles goes to the head, sits down on the toilet,
and lets go. Pees, for the first time he can remember, sitting
down. A full bladder and a sense of relief as if all these years
of standing to pee there was something pinched in the core
of him. Miles listens to his urine splash on the stainless-steel
flap. Then he flushes. Flushes and, although he knows the
waste goes into a tank to be drained later, he imagines the
urine going straight out into the Arctic Ocean. And then he
is there again, cruising the currents with the sea lions and
narwhals, with that fortunate minke—harpoon-scarred but
healing—and the other quietly bobbing giants of the deep.

The summer before his father left for good, Miles stayed up
listening to a screaming match—his father bellowing "Bitch!"
into the ceiling like the name of some profane god and his
mother hissing "why don't you hit me then you big man."
Miles alone in his bedroom weeping as cupboards rattled and
plates clanged and then in the morning his father walked into
the living room with a big white box in a semi-opaque *Sears*
bag, the beautiful Nintendo oval showing through.

Miles revelled in *Super Mario*. Spent his nights dreaming
of giant mushrooms, made snowballs fancying that he would
jiep-jiep-jiep up a size and begin tossing fireballs. But it was
his father who grew to be consumed by the game. Became a
terrible TV-room vampire, began to spend his nights with a
glass of scotch he never seemed to drink from and the music
blaring about the dark and flickering walls. Within weeks the
man had beaten the game several times and knew all the short-
cuts. But he kept playing, began playing for points. Trying to
beat the game as fast as he could without losing a life. His face
growing paler and paler and Miles' mother coming in to cut
him off, her voice low and urgent. The awful music looping
through the night until their dreams were filled with flying

fish and gombas travelling blue underworlds. Until Miles would get up and stagger through the dark halls, lit with slanted red and blue, glancing into the TV room to see if the tinny synthesizer symphony was in fact coming from there or if it was just looping—*boing, boing, boing*—through the twisting pseudo-tropical funhouse that had become his mind.

In the early days, before Miles' father got fully addicted to *Super Mario*, he and Miles had once beaten a level together. A level that had always been Miles' favourite—the underwater level, where Mario is a strange sea-creature, a human body with a fishtail. Seven-year-old Miles and his father sat there playing level life and the gruff old Nazi was momentatily gentle. Gentle and patient and tender as they blooped through the pixelated blue.

When they finally won, his father stood up and turned the TV off. Said it was always best to end on a good note, and walked out into the kitchen to make them both a Nutella sandwich but don't tell your mother. His father eating his sandwich with his mouth closed and a grin in his eyes, a grin Miles had never seen before. A smear of hazelnut butter in his white moustache.

Miles walks into the torpedo room and finds Panchaud doing crunches, stomach twitching through his blue navy shirt. A row of teeth under a layer of chewing gum. The XO looks up at Miles, not pausing his workout. His feet locked under the rail below the torpedo tube and his elbows twisting one way then the other, gently kissing the opposite knee before gliding back down to rest. His elbows like wings.

Miles lies down beside the XO. Hooks his feet under the same rail but does not rise into a crunch. Instead, he listens to the man's breathing. The hush and shush of its rise and fall. He feels the heat swelling out from that hard body and he listens for the song in the man's breath. In through the nose, out through the mouth. The breaths getting shorter, thicker, and finally stopping as Panchaud collapses onto the floor.

Miles leans onto his side and puts a palm on the XO's stomach. Feels the firm ridges and valleys of that waffle-like grid. A stomach like a flattened city.

"It's tough," Miles says. "Down here."

Panchaud looking back at him, his brown eyes a hatred. A confusion. A longing.

"All of this—it's really hard."

Panchaud keeps looking back at him. Miles reaches out and the two men take each other's hands. Miles can feel Panchaud's rapid pulse through his fingertips. Can feel the slight lilt of his hand as Panchaud's chest rises and falls—the struggle in his breath slowing, slowing, done.

Entering the next screen, Miles and his aqueous cartoon father encounter something strange: a tall rectangle swaying gently in the digital current. A rectangle that, as they bloop closer, reveals itself to be a skyscraper. A once-glorious skyscraper of human construction, rising up from the ocean floor. Empty windows clogged with algae and the once-gleaming stones studded with barnacles. Ancient roadways spiralling upwards and cluttered with the rusted remnants of cars, all of it less sinister than it should be, gleaming with the primary palate of cartoons.

They are just about to reach the underwater city when a bad guy emerges from behind one of the buildings. A giant human-squid hybrid with a stump leg and a pirate's eye patch. Puffing a cigar, a swirl of oil rising up where the smoke should be.

The squid produces a rocket launcher. Sets it on his shoulder and fires. The missile soars impossibly through the black water. Twists and lurches and careers as only a video game heat-seeker could and Miles can see that the weapon has smelled him. The missile hot and snarling and near and then Miles says it:

"Activate."

He says "Activate" and everything goes still. The heat-seeker goes flaccid, disperses into sea. The squid squirts a swirling jet stream of black ink and shrinks into its vortex. The water ceases to warble and all sound effects stop. His father tells him he is sorry. Not, as usual, sorry about the Botox humiliation or ever agreeing to christen his only son "Miles." He is sorry, now, for withholding. Sorry he could not have been nicer to Miles or his mother. Sorry and he often wished he could but he simply couldn't do it. Says all this and then he too vanishes into the squid's inky whirlpool.

His father wilts into liquid nothing and Miles finds himself alone in the cavernous dark thinking about crush depth, about the pressure clutching this ship like a great fist, a whole ocean waiting to squash this arrogant vessel and send fifty-eight seamen drifting through the deep. Which is when he conjures his mother. Remembers his mother and knows that although she is gone she also remains. And so he sits there on the toilet and says it again: "Activate." Holds his palms up to brush the air around him and feels the power of this little bubble of safety in a world always threatening to infiltrate. For what else is life but a fragile island in the chaos, a bulwark against the storms and oceans always gathering to subsume us?

LIMOUSINES

Dale kept asking are you sure about going through with it and I kept telling him they said level one cyclone which means it'll be downgraded to dry-heaving tropical storm. I didn't imagine myself standing here sluicing liquid reek in front of all my loved ones while the deadstock truck squeaks and teeters towards me, dust wafting about its crown of pretzelled limbs. Dad didn't want a preacher on his property and so it's just the judge and me and Dale and the deadstock truck creaking over the horizon like a goblin chariot roofed with a thatch of cadavers.

Dad springs out of his lawn chair and starts waving fury at the truck until it turns around. The truck he'd told not to come if it couldn't make it by two p.m. and it's 5:30 now. The truck that was supposed to pick up two Holsteins who died of septic infection yesterday and are now reeking and gas-bloated behind Uncle Stan's pig barn. The vehicle's three-point turn full of *reet-reet-reets* and everyone watching that knot of carcasses wobble and lurch as the judge speaks about the ancient covenant of matrimony. The corset of my strapless dress bunched tight up top to maximize cleavage and I never noticed until I looked into the mirror five minutes before walking the grass-and-mud aisle but the squeezing means there's a slit like a butt crack down the middle of my upper back, a gob of sweat cradled in its uppermost estuary.

As the judge drones her spiel—legal stuff plus something about harmony and a never-ending web—I watch the deadstock truck bounce back down the farm drive, a stiff menagerie strapped to its back. Above that tangle of fur and hoof and rigor mortis, the sky is thick with the promise of storm. But the storm still seems to be holding. Holding meaning no wind or rain yet, just a slick and vicious heat, a humidity rare in this grid of hayfields and ocean breeze.

We say "I do," walk past the front pasture towards the old barn.

We do cocktails and dinner in the old barn. Sit with the smell of hay and dead mice, drinking dark and stormies. Or as Dale calls them, stark and dormies. Salty smoke wafts in from outside where Uncle Stan slings pork-related innuendos in his bikini-bod apron while tending to the gilt he's been roasting over coal for what seems like a week.

Dad stands up in front of everyone and tells Dale to pay close attention because he's going to give him some words to live by, namely: "Never take a sleeping pill and a laxative at the same time." Dad grins wide—three upper teeth floating in a pudding of black—and I do my best not to think too hard about what he's said. Then Dad gives his characteristic double-eyed wink and says in his joking-but-not-really tone, "By the way I slipped some Cialis in your cocktail so I expect some grandbabies in nine months' time."

A gush of wind through the barn and I will the thunder to crack but it doesn't. Dale and I look at each other and then I look away quickly, hoping nobody noticed but knowing everybody noticed.

Uncle Stan walks in swinging his hips and calls out that the meat's ready so form a line before Dale gets to it. Everyone gathers out back holding out their plates for slabs of tasty pink with Stan's famous maple syrup glaze. The smoky flesh slicking onto paper plates as Dale and I smile wide for the well-wishers. The word "grandbabies" sharp in our ears.

The storm holds and the storm holds and around one the storm breaks. A warm-cored, non-frontal synoptic with sixty-kilometer-per-hour winds leaving it just a gust or two outside of level one. Meaning the storm remains nameless, another anonymous tropical. Most of the guests stay in the old barn drinking the rest of the hard liquor or stumbling over to Uncle Stan's for a midnight pork feast while Dale and I spend our wedding night lying awake with the music of the storm punctuated by Angie and Lloyd ruddering headboard into wall. Dale and I clutching each other and listening to the boom and howl and skittle of the storm and beneath it the wails of drunk love like ghosts in the wall. Angie and Lloyd in the room right over ours and hard to say which one of them is doing the moaning. "Jesus," Dale says at one point. "What is he, a goddamn jackrabbit?"

Then we hear a worrying boom and Dale sits up straight in bed but when Angie starts cackling we realize it was just the mattress sliding off the old plank bed and Dale and I start to laugh too. Laugh and clutch each other tighter and then the storm really musters, crackles and clangs across the field and the cows take up a chorus, belting and screaming, their voices like glue, yoking the pattering raindrops.

Dale asks if I want to go see them and I say sure. So we put on rain gear and squelch out through the blasting night and down to the big barn where the cows are still howling and kicking at the walls. The lights are on and Dad's already down there walking from stall to stall with the curry brush. He looks at us with his toothless grin and says we're morons to leave the house. He's got the Sailor Jerry out and we pass it around before walking through the stalls giving the cows grass and rubbing their backs, murmuring gently in their ears.

"What a honeymoon," Dale says on our way back up to the house. He says it was a lovely honeymoon and I tell him yes, tell him it was perfect. Tell him and almost mean it.

Dale asks for the Honey Nut Cheerios and I slide them down the table. It's been two days since the wedding and the power's still out. The deadstock truck hasn't been able to get back yet so those two dead Holsteins remain behind Uncle Stan's pig barn, a yellowing horror of bloat and gas. A tree fell on the back pasture fence but there was no real damage to the property or the livestock. Just a troupe of soaked wedding guests unable to get taxis or drive home so all of them slept in the barn or the house or over at Uncle Stan's. In the morning a ham breakfast for fifty people and then everyone drove home stopping to haul the scattered branches and tufts of hay bale off the dirt road.

Dale pours a full bowl of Cheerios, fuller than usual, then asks about my period. I tell him everything's normal and he nods, slurps at his milk. Even smiles with his eyes a little as he looks at me over the rim of the bowl. When you're trying to get pregnant, and especially when you're struggling to get pregnant, your period becomes a subject at breakfast table conversation. You find yourself telling your long-term companion things you never realized you'd been keeping secret. Like the fact that when you were thirteen the family collie, Oedipus Rex, used to snatch your sanitary napkins out from the bathroom garbage. Used to strut them into the living room for public munching and sit there snarfing until you walked in to find your father just standing there looking down at the dog. Standing there frozen and when he saw you he looked up and said he was sorry and he always did his best but he simply had no clue how to deal with this.

So Dale asks about my period and I tell him no baby and he says okay, reaches out and touches my arm. Usually when I tell Dale I got my period he looks at me like I've just snapped off the big section of a wishbone which is also his penis. But now he seems tender and sweet, which makes me suspect something is wrong and then feel terrible that this is where my mind goes.

I play Scrabble on my phone while Dale finishes his breakfast. Then he hobbles over to the sink and puts his cereal bowl in without rinsing it. Dale's legs are two different lengths so his walk is more of a hobble but he is a good man with a big heart. If anything too big. Not sure why but I imagine his heart as a football. I think if I pulled it out of his chest and tossed it along a patch of turf, it would bounce in the same warped, unpredictable way.

"Out of milk," Dale says. "Want to go see Guinan?"

Why did Dale go suddenly antsy about marriage after ten years living together on Dad's farm? Presumably it had something to do with the conception troubles. After two years of trying I got myself checked out and Doctor Spencer said I was "better than normal" and so it stood to reason that Dale's sperm was the issue. I tried but couldn't tell Dale this so I told him the doctor had said I had an abnormal uterus and it was unlikely. Dale went dull-eyed and said "let's just keep trying" and I was worried he'd break up with me and find someone more fertile which would have been messy and wrong. But he didn't break up with me. Instead, he waited a week or two and said about marriage. We were watching *P.S. I Love You* and he said, "Let's do it," his eyes wet with wonder. He said we should get married and I said as long as we don't do engagement photos or a garter toss. Dale grinned and said that was too bad because he'd really been looking forward to tossing his garter. He'd had a good feeling Uncle Stan would be the one to catch it.

The big, boxy Limos are out in the front pasture as we walk down to see Guinan. Twenty-five cows and a dozen calves and the bull, Warf, is out too, feasting alone in the back corner. We're traditionally a dairy farm but Dad has always kept some beef cows for hobby breeding and extra cash, hence the Limousines. They're technically called *Limousin* after the French region but my father always called these exotics "Limos" or "Limousines" so that's how I think of them. As a girl I'd wished that they were extra long, with a third set of legs.

Limos are known for their lean, tasty beef and for being ornery or, in Dad's words, "European." They're naturally horned but Dad takes those off, the horns, when they're infants, castrating the calves at the same time. They've got an angular figure and colouration ranging from buttermilk to earthy red to pure black. Dale and I recently watched that Herzog movie and I was struck by how much the 20,000-year-old rock paintings in the Great Hall of the Bulls look like Limousines—same big, square shoulders, same earthen, monochrome coat.

The Limos bound over to the edge of the fence, a few of their tails raised and bent from being recently bred. Dale hitches over to the fence on his uneven legs and feeds some grass to the new calves, Zorn and Deanna. Dad gives all his cows names from *Star Trek*—he started with the original series and now he's up to *Next Generation*.

As we walk into her little room beside the chickens, Guinan trots over, her udders bulging and her wet snout alive with snorts. Cat Stevens and Margaret Catwood are already purring around our ankles. Dale gets the curry brush and rubs Guinan's flank as I grab the bucket and give Guinan's huge Holstein udders a few soft pats to let the milk down. Most of the cows get milked on the mechanical milking platform but we keep Guinan for the family and take the milk naturally because nothing tastes better. By the time I've put a few long squirts into the bucket Cat Stevens and Margaret Catwood are howling around my ankles so I tilt the two teats I'm holding and the barn cats sit back and open their mouths as the spurts *siss* through the air—the milk splashing off their skulls and chins and the cats with their eyes closed lapping at the air.

A week after the wedding Dale and I head into the city to return some wedding gifts and when we get back it looks like there's been a flash storm. There was no warning and no trace of it in Halifax but the county road is slick with rain and there's a post-storm shudder in the air.

As we grind down the farm road I see the vet's truck and what looks like a mound of sandy dirt in the middle of the front pasture. A mound of sandy dirt with some black patches. A mound that grows dimensions as we get closer. A mound that congeals into a huddle of immobile bodies, a cluster of lifeless Limousines.

Eight or ten of them under the big oak which is missing a large, blackened limb. I park the truck and slide out the door into the hideous haze of the Limousines' death-gas. Then I see Dad talking to the vet while he saws through the leg of a cow. Taking a Gigli saw to the animal's thigh and working through that death-stiffened limb in the open field. A dead Limousine cow and the red-headed vet in knee-high rubber boots tells me pantingly that he has to saw open the leg to determine the cause of death. Tells me he'll also have to take tissue samples and perform a necropsy to make sure the animals were not diseased. The vet tells me it's just an insurance issue and largely a formality but I am not listening as I look down at about fifteen tons of dead and reeking animal. There are nine of them—Jarth, Liva, Farallon, Yareena, Lutan, Kayron, Regina, Aquiel, and Toreth. Nine soft giant creatures lying dead in the grass where they ate and bred and lived and I can see in Dad's face that he is angry but also wounded.

The vet gets in his truck and me, Dad, and Dale head inside to make coffee. Dad stirs cream into his cup and sits there for a long time before taking a sip. Finally he sniffs hard and says what a bitch this will be what with the paperwork and having to get the deadstock truck back. I tell him yeah, I know what he means. I know what he means.

Although Dad uses artificial insemination for the Holsteins he keeps a bull, Warf, for the Limos.

You might think the life of a lone bull on a farm with twenty to twenty-five cows would be glorious. The moaning suggests otherwise. The moaning suggests torture. The bull only gets put out for two or three months at a time during summer. Otherwise there's not much point, financially, in exercising the bull and you can't have him around the cows. So what we hear all winter is Warf lowing forlornly, bleating out his pain and longing. The lonely, sex-starved bull getting no relief and sometimes fucking the wall of his stall until his penis is chafed and bloody.

The next night I drive Dale to the airport and when we get there he kisses me gently, his eyes whispering "maybe you'll be ovulating when I'm back." Dale is a millwright, and though I've asked him many times I'm still not sure exactly what a millwright does. Even the word seems unhelpful and old-timey. Dale works fourteen fourteen which means getting on the same Seaboard Air flight every two weeks, the flight they call the gasoline limousine, the flight that lands in Edmonton where the men line up for the shuttle north to Fort Mac, where they line up to swipe into their weird little hotels and then line up to swipe their cards for dinner, for break, for the gym or the little private movie theatre. Dale works fourteen fourteen and I stay home and fix little metal mouths onto cow nipples. At night I watch *Star Trek* with Dad and work on my meteorology blog and plan our trip to Arizona that will probably never happen while wasting pregnancy test after pregnancy test. When he's home the milking gets a little easier and I spend half my life on my back, holding my legs up like a strung turkey.

I put Dale on the gasoline limousine and when I get home the sun is fully down and I can feel the great slurs of the Holsteins lolling through the darkness in the front pasture. The lights are on in the barn and Dad's down there blasting Van Halen so I park the truck and head down to join him. Dad's in the back changing a tire on the tractor, screaming along to "Smokin' in the Boy's Room." He can't hear me over the music so I pick up his bottle of Sailor Jerry and wait for him to reach for it. He lets his hand dangle where the bottle should be for a long time, then looks up at me beaming, his teeth like strange square stars in the blackness of his mouth.

I ask him how's it going and he says, as he has every time I've asked him this question over the past thirty-one years, "Not bad for an old fella." Then he rises up off the mat he'd been kneeling on, turns off the Van Halen, and asks if I want to help him bring in the girls.

So we bring in the girls. Open the back barn doors and breathe the rich tannin smell of the pasture as it washes through. The smell you get used to but never stop smelling. The smell you miss when you're in the city the way you'd miss your nose if it weren't there when you glanced down at your chest.

We head out into the pasture where I ring the bell and Dad shouts the cow call, "co-boss." I've never asked what it means and I don't ask now. Although they usually stay out all night or come in on their own around 6 p.m. they know what's going on. The girls troop through with their bellows and groans and their big dark tender eyes. Eyes in all their varieties of brown, rich and nourishing as the hum of manure.

Dad and I close their stalls and start to brush them off. When they're all in and settled we sit down with the Sailor Jerry and Dad raises the bottle and says, "To the poor creatures who died today." We both take a drink and then sit there for a while thinking of those cows hunched under the tree, of the vet sawing through Farallon's massive thigh.

Finally Dad says as he often does how strange it is that there are 1.5 billion cattle in the world. He says think about all those city folks that never get close enough to smell one. 1.5 billion of these quiet creatures living in secret on the far side of the city walls, a whole bovine underground that keeps their beef-and-milk world turning.

"Or something like that," he adds.

We sit listening to the cows groaning and snorting, to the quiet suckling of calves. Then Dad pats me on the shoulder and says, "Well Laura: two more weeks, just me and the girls." He grins. "Could be worse eh?"

I tell him yeah it could, and although he needs to make it seem like a joke I also know he means it. And I mean it too.

I remember five or six years ago walking over to my uncle's place and finding him guiding a pig into a sow. I stood there for some time gasping and watching and struggling to believe that in this age of mechanized farming a man would still stand overtop of a pig and manually assist him with intercourse. My uncle was not even wearing gloves. I saw everything. I saw the black hairs on my uncle's pinky. I saw the pig on his hind legs and his thin curlicued cock steaming in the December chill and my uncle reaching down and grasping that slick digit between thumb and forefinger, sending it in. I turned away out of embarrassment and pretended to be interested in some of last year's shoats but the truth was they were no longer cute. My uncle trotted up to me, gloating in my discomfort, and said there was nothing to worry about, said it was perfectly normal. He said animals didn't get embarrassed about that kind of thing and I thought *but what about you?* He said don't worry, that I'd get to do that too when I was all grown up. I told him that was inappropriate on so many levels and he grinned as if this were a compliment.

Dale has a lovely crooked heart and yet here I am. It was easy to find a man online. What was more difficult was finding a man who would go with me to the doctor's for an STI test and then hand me the paperwork. I couldn't trust anyone I know and so I ended up with Duke, the beetle-faced ex-navy man with clean medical records and stellar teeth. Nearly forty years older than me and he has to wear this certain type of sock that helps his veins to circulate but none of that affects the semen or the genetics. Duke has a good IQ score and no twins or heart conditions or dementia in the family and his eyes are the same pale blue as Dale's. Eyes that I keep trying to meet as he works on top of me, eyes that I search for, trying to find Dale in them, trying to swerve this moment into some kind of love. But it's not love. It's not love and maybe it never has been. After Duke finishes he looks over my head and says, "Thank you." Says it as if he's thanking something holy, something much greater than me.

It is relatively rare, in the era of modern medical science, for a woman to die in childbirth. But it happens. It happens that some trace amounts of amniotic fluid trickle through the woman's placental bed and enter the bloodstream. Happens that this episode of amniotic fluid embolism goes unnoticed by medical staff and that the woman leaves the hospital after an apparently successful and routine pregnancy. That this woman complains later that night of abdominal pains and strange pressure. It happens that a man drives his wife back to the hospital with his brother in the backseat holding the brand-new screaming infant. Happens that the mother dies right there in the car of a sudden cardiorespiratory collapse. Asphyxiates and stops breathing. Loses her pulse there on the shoulder of the highway with her husband offering mouth to mouth and twelve-hour-old baby Laura wailing in her uncle's arms. It happens that the doctor tells this man that there was nothing anyone could have done and the man knows this is supposed to make him feel better but it does not tame the storm rising in him.

Dad is somewhat antiquated in that he lets his cows eat grass as much as possible—most dairy farmers just give them corn and alfalfa. Dad was doing all this stuff anyway but about fifteen years ago a niche market developed for grass-fed dairy, so Dad joined a cooperative and now most of our milk goes towards artisanal cheeses. But in spite of the whole organic-pastoral fantasy, we do not milk the cows by hand. We milk the Holsteins on the mechanical milking platform Dad had installed in the nineties, and though I've been watching it happen for twenty years I still find it strange to see those giddy cows lining up to get little metal leeches latched onto their udders. Sometimes I wonder what they're thinking as the teatcups suckle them, draining their maternal fluid into the vacuum and onwards to the bulk tank. I wonder if they think about their children. If, maybe, they have faith that we are keeping their babies somewhere safe. That once they drain their milk we deliver it to their children, who are still living close by, somewhere just out of sight.

I didn't want to tell my news over the phone and apparently neither did Dale. Because we're sitting in the truck on the way home from the airport and I'm just about to mention about the pregnancy when he says he got laid off. Turning up the long exit ramp with a pair of bastard-bright halogens in my rear-view and Dale blurts that he's out of work. His voice pale and wounded and I look over for his eyes but can't find them in the vehicular dark.

He tells me he's been laid off and he's not sure what he'll do but somebody knows somebody at the new shipyard and I say it's okay. I say it's not the time, hoping he'll think I mean not the time to worry about money or employment when really I mean not the time to say about the child. A new child and its father out of work and he always said I was supposed to stay home and help Dad chip away at his debt while Dale made the money and now what?

When we get home Dad's already in bed which means Dale has one beer and a quick shot of whiskey while I nurse a peppermint tea. Dale tells me he thinks they were stupid, those Limousines. He thinks they were stupid for huddling together under a tree where they're basically begging to be hit by lightning. I know he loves the cattle, too, but I have to wonder how a man could spend so many years with these creatures and think them stupid. I tell him I think there's something awful and lovely in this kind of death—cattle lying together under a tree and the lightning coming down and all of them going at once. He shrugs, unconvinced, and says he's tired.

In bed, Dale stays up watching *American Horror Story* on his laptop and I lie next to him pretending to sleep, thinking about the man in the scree dune. The smell of the ocean and the gentle rub of the plaid blanket under my hips. I think of the whish of the ocean and the seagulls barking their tuneless dirge and the man panting and panting until his breath became the ocean and the ocean was entering me.

I keep thinking I should turn over and tell Dale I'm pregnant but I don't. Instead, I fall asleep thinking about the dead Limousin cattle. I see the nine of them prancing on the walls of the Great Hall of the Bulls, which I saw recently in that Herzog movie. They're on the wall of the cave but they aren't all coarse and ochre-coloured like the petroglyphs. They're more like how they are in real life—boxy frames and pale brown coats, the strange moss where their horns were cut off and cauterized. And they're dancing. Swaying gently back and forth on the wall, one of them with a leg cut off cleanly above the knee.

About a year ago Dale and I were walking out to observe a rare nacreous cloud formation and a few minutes after we'd been walking along the rim of a cornfield this man appeared holding a shotgun. A bearded man wearing cut-off jean-shorts, his shins stark white. Usually we stayed on our side of the river but on this day we'd decided to cross and we were just ambling along the edge of the field staring up at the honey pouring through those strange flat clouds when there was a sawed-off twenty feet from us and behind it a man in garrison boots and ragged jean-shorts, his whole body a growl.

"The fuck out of here," he said. His beard gaped open, his mouth perverse in its wetness.

Dale said okay, take it easy, we're going. Took my arm and led me away. Dale squeezed my hand almost viciously and I was thinking but not wanting to say goodbye. The distant *shish* of the starlings and the creek's soft gush and we were almost home before my heart settled somewhat, before I stopped thinking with every step that my back or brain might be suddenly opened by a rage of buckshot.

We never saw any pot plants but what else could it have been? After that, Dale and I headed in the other direction when we took our walks along the creek, but things were never the same. I never told Dad because he wouldn't like it, might even try to get involved. But for me it was crazy to think about your neighbours out there, ready to pull a shotgun on you. Awful to think that if they wanted to they could cross the creek and come down here at night. But mostly it was just terrible to think, to really think about what a shotgun blast would do to your body, how it could instantly trade the fragile fiction of form for the honest muck of flesh.

Twice a year or so Dad fills up a trailer with the Limousines that are ready for the abattoir, the fats. We don't see the actual death, which is good but also weird. Weird because afterwards the farm seems far more quiet than the missing bovine voices should leave it. Weird because Dad sometimes recycles the fats' *Star Trek* names when new calves are born. Weird because if you know anything about slaughterhouses you can't help picturing and maybe dreaming about these companions being skinned, eviscerated, and sawed in two lengthwise. Weird because cows form profound emotional bonds, particularly among females, and so the new quietude around the farm after the fats have been sent to the abattoir feels a lot like a big bruise purpling in the mammatus clouds that loom over the farm.

Wearing full rubber suits and white disposable masks, Dad, Dale, and Uncle Stan pick up the piglets and smash their heads into the concrete floor before toeing them to make sure they're dead. Slamming their skulls into the concrete and trampling through the gore to toss the little ragdoll corpses into barrels to become slop. The smell is an enormity of rot—fecund and noxious. Stan called the house after waking up this morning to find his ninety-three piglets puking and spasming in the dirt, their mothers walking around milk-swelled and groaning. We got the vet over and learned that the mothers and babies all had some kind of stomach infection and that the only way to cure it was to cull the piglets and feed them back to their mothers.

I said I'd come down to help with the cleanup and I want to help because all of us know it is awful but it needs to be done. But I can't help. Can't even watch and yet I am watching. Watching brains lather concrete and my father and Uncle Stan looking focused, set on the task. They are not enjoying it but they seem to take a certain satisfaction in doing it right.

Dale does not look focused. Dale looks wrecked. Dale stands there holding one spasming baby pig by the legs and raising it up and just looking at it rapt, as if he could will it to heal. He looks like he would like to take it into his arms, to cradle it like a human infant.

Dad and Stan trade a glance and everyone feels their meaning.

"Dale," Dad says. "Either do it or get out of here."

So Dale raises the piglet slowly. Raises it and holds it high and then brings it down. Dale swings the piglet hard and fast but wavers halfway. Slows the swing so that the piglet doesn't die, only lies there still spasming with a dent in its head.

Dale looks at me then. Meets my eyes as he stands uselessly over the still shuddering baby pig and I choose this time to say that I'm pregnant. Dale is the only one who hears. My father standing behind him holding two freshly killed baby pigs and Dale quivering as I repeat that I'm pregnant. Stan walks over and picks up the dented pig and does what needs to be done, blood splatting onto my pant leg. Dale walks forward holding out his blood-browned arms as if to hug me, his face an agony of joy.

Before cattle are slaughtered for beef they go into something called a squeeze chute, part of a system pioneered by behaviourist Temple Grandin. Cattle are prey animals and they don't like loud noises or carnivores like humans standing where they can't see them. The squeeze chute closes in around them and hugs them, making them feel safe while they ride down the conveyor towards their electric demise. A similar machine can be used to calm hypersensitive people, but when used on humans it's called a "hug machine." And isn't there something nice in that, something sweet in the thought that in their last moments cattle are taken into a set of great metallic arms and hugged to death?

In bed that night Dale seems to have forgotten all about the pigs. He keeps patting my belly and trying to see if I'm showing yet and I tell him no way. I tell him it'll be another eight weeks before anything like that and there's still a fifty percent chance of miscarriage but none of it darkens his bliss. We look at a pregnancy app together and it shows us an image of the fetus at five weeks, looking like a little tadpole feeding on a yolk sac twice its size. It has translucent skin and looks strangely reptilian. Dale leans down and whispers into my belly, calling the baby "Taddy" and "Radpole" and "Lizzy the Wizard."

After Dale falls asleep I stand up and walk to the window, look out over the pasture where the Holsteins are passing the night. I can't see them clearly but I can sense their black, hulking forms and I think about pastures, think about the new slick monopoly operation down the road. Me and Dad were driving yesterday and we saw that they'd finished the construction and looked to be starting business. I stared at that roofed aluminum city thinking something was strange with it. We were three clicks away before I blurted, "Where were the pastures?"

Dad told me they didn't have pastures, the new dairy farms. Pastures weren't efficient so the animals simply stayed inside. Stayed in ten-by-six stalls with milk machine robots travelling between them and just pumping, pumping. I think of that strange giant barn all full of cows being suckled by machines, their calves sent off for veal and their milk being sucked, and my breasts start to throb. There's been some pain from contact but nothing like this—a huge and unprovoked ache. As if my breasts were trapped souls, howling.

Below, the Holsteins plod through their private, outdoor lives. Some of them loafing about, some of them eating, most lying down to sleep. One of them groans and I wonder what she's saying. Is she lost or lonely, does she miss her calf? Or is she just saying hello, just sending her voice into the world? Whatever she's saying, I can't imagine not hearing it. Can't imagine looking out this window and not seeing cows in the pasture. Can't and don't want to imagine growing up on a farm with no hulking shadows loafing through the dark.

I sit at the edge of the mattress and graze my knuckles across Dale's forehead. I don't say it aloud but just sort of think towards him that I'm glad he couldn't do it, happy he couldn't kill those baby pigs. He twitches and sleep-wheezes. Mutters something incoherent, something I can't quite understand. Something verging on word in the tenderest of tones.

DRIFT

Julie is standing in the Queen Street Sobeys when the announcement comes over the PA. She's receiving a slab of pork from the avuncular red-nosed butcher and she suddenly becomes aware that she is holding a hunk of dead animal body. Flesh that was recently growing, twitching. Flesh that had been weary, sated, sore. The Sobeys regional whatever clears his throat and says *East Rock*, says *methane*, says *rescue effort*, and she can feel the coldness of the pork tenderloin through its clay-red jacket. She is thinking *no*, thinking *fucksakes*, thinking *not now*. Recalling Lorne at six, his hockey goon grin as she helped him write his name again and again on the back cover of their father's yachting magazine. Showing her that he could do it himself and yes he could do it perfectly except he made the capital "L" backwards every time. She conjures the scrawl of his reverted "L," perturbed shoppers drifting by like receipts in a subway station.

And then she is home. She is in her home on Victoria Road, walking up to Franz, feeling less like a person or a body than a shuddering field of static and nerve. Franz is eating olives and holding a rolled-up newspaper and he hugs her without needing to ask why and it's only then that she realizes she did not pay for the tenderloin. She stole that cut of meat and she is squeezing it now, squeezing as if death were not a question, as if the warmth of her hands could reanimate that flesh, squeezing heedless of the blood seeping through the butcher's paper, pocking the white tiles of her kitchen floor.

She tells Franz what she heard at Sobeys and he gently pulls the tenderloin out of her hand, places it in the sink. He helps her over to the couch and pours a glass of Perrier that she doesn't lift from the walnut coffee table. She watches a ring form. She stares and stares at that ghost-white halo and thinks of her brother getting his front teeth pulled. Remembers how she and her mother had sat together in the dentist's office clutching magazines and listening to his screams blaring through the dentist's door. The sound of the drill and her brother screaming and there was nothing she could do. He came out with a black square in the front of his face and he had no recollection of the pain. Did not remember screaming and was happy to bring his tongue up into that new slimy cavity and stare at himself in the elevator mirror.

"Should we go?" Franz asks.

"No," she says. "He's fine. I'm sure he's fine."

She heads to the phone and calls her brother's home number and of course he doesn't answer—she spoke to him last night and knows he was on shift this morning. But she calls again just to listen to his voice on the answering machine, asking her to please leave a message.

They are biking up Chebucto Road beneath a blaring sun. They are climbing the hill on their way to Chocolate Lake and it has always been an unspoken pact that they pedal as fast as they can, that they arrive at the lake sweaty and panting and race straight into the water, let it shock them into mute euphoria.

Her calves stiffen and she digs harder, churning the pedals, but the hill does not mellow. She feels the pavement soften in the heat, her tires slugging through the gummy black. The sun fierce on her shoulders and she longs for water, yearns to watch the trees hang over the shore, green and gentle in the light lake breeze.

She can sense her brother now, too close behind her. She pumps her thighs, racing less against him than against her own fear of being caught. He whizzes past on the outside, raises his middle finger and looks over his shoulder, a jagged thrill in his eyes. Which is when she learns there is another gear in her. She clamps down and the pedals lighten. Her tires dig and chuck and she is gone, past him again and this time he will not overtake her.

Eventually Jack and Owen come inside panting from their street hockey game and sensing in their childish way that something is wrong. They are sweaty and beautiful, blue eyes gleaming out of their cinnamon skin and she is filled with a nausea of love. They sit down on the couch beside her. Sit in a perfect silence she would never be able to command.

After a hushed explanation to the boys, Franz puts the radio on and they wait for news. They wait one hour, then two. They wait for names, long for names. Names of the missing, the rescued, the buried, the people who were down in the drifts when the methane swelled and surged and blasted. The reporters say "ambulances," "rescue," "draegermen." But there are no names. No facts. No news. No mention of 1838, 1880, 1958—each endeavour ending in methane, in explosion.

She calls her brother three more times, this time hanging up before the machine answers, riding the ring's sonic purr as if that bleating song could lull the real. Owen ventures into the yard and returns with a bouquet of dandelions and how could she not turn to liquid, smile and start to weep as she oozes into her son's arms?

Franz overcooks the tenderloin and they eat dinner early, hunched around the television, still desperate for news and getting nothing. The meat is chewy with too much savoury glaze but Julie insists that they eat the whole thing. She and the boys sit wordless at the table listening to the radio, chewing slow and dutiful, jaws tired. She keeps chewing long after Franz and the boys have given up, their brows brailled with sweat. Julie eats that Sobeys pork like secular eucharist, eats as if all her love for her brother were bent into this task, eats until the plate is bare and pink and her husband's eyes are a bluster of worry.

Still no news from the radio. No names. No dead. No survivors.

The pork in her mouth ceases to be meat, becomes flesh.

Coal is sedimentary rock formed from peat that has been crushed and condensed over hundreds of millions of years. It is derived from plant matter that flourished about 325 million years ago during the carboniferous period and was subsequently covered by layers of sediment and cooked slowly through the ages. Though China is the world leader in coal extraction and production, many regions worldwide still mine coal and use it as part of their energy grids. Nova Scotia Power currently operates four facilities—Lingan, Point Aconi, Point Tupper, and Trenton—that use coal or pet coke to generate electricity.

Lorne shouts from behind her but she leans on the handlebars and keeps pedalling. The hill yields, curves, and begins to send her down, down towards the Rotary and the Northwest Arm. She pedals and pedals and stops, lets the bike tilt into the hill and carry her down. Sunlight winking off windshields and behind them the glimmer of the Northwest Arm, the blue sky blooming popcorn clouds.

A sustained horn blares and Lorne shrieks again and this time there is a quaver in his voice. Something is wrong but she's going too fast to look back. Brakes screeching and her brother crying out and she cannot stop the bicycle fast enough, finds herself jumping off. Rolling onto grass, then pavement.

Julie rises and looks back up the hill to where her brother lies on the road next to two pickups with their four-ways on. Distress and burnt rubber shimmering in the sunlight. Lorne's red Supercycle crumpled beneath a tire and Lorne on the ground, clinging to his leg and wailing.

She sets off up the hill towards him.

After dinner she rises wordlessly and heads upstairs to pack. She takes a quiet pleasure in the sound of the zipper of her toiletries case, in the sponge of her socks as she folds them into her suitcase. She senses herself trying to slow things down, to cultivate the drawl of ritual. When she comes downstairs with her bags, Franz asks where she's going and she simply looks at him. He nods, rises, and begins to herd the boys and their overnight bags into the Camry. He calls work for her, says maybe a week, maybe more. Then he calls her parents in Vancouver and tells them to book a flight. He looks at her like "do you want to" and she shakes her head like "I just can't." Hanging up, he says her parents have booked a flight, they'll be there by tomorrow night.

They drive through the saline twilight of the 102 while the boys nod into their soft oblivions and Julie stays terribly alert, watching for the wildlife she half-expects to dart into the road. They arrive at the site around nine, a floodlight cast over the scene, and find a fleet of ambulances and media and a man in an orange vest telling everyone to go home. He uses his best gym teacher voice but there is fear in the pallor of his face, worry limning his deep-set eyes. He is saying "twenty-six," saying "draegermen," saying "all's we know." She takes far too long to decode that there are twenty-six men underground. She pushes up and tries not to scream but hears her voice wail like a trapped housecat as she asks after her brother. Asks after her brother when of course she already knows, has known from the moment the announcement came over the PA: he is down there. He is down there buried and alone and there is nothing she can do to help him. The man in the vest says yes Lorne was reported below ground at the time of explosion and that's all he can say.

She walks to the edge of the police tape and looks out towards the shaft. Men with headlamps huddle there, readying themselves to enter a cavern that exploded mere hours before. Preparing to brave that darkness to rescue her brother. She wonders how deep she would go to save him. Would she climb down the shaft and dig through the debris of that blasted cavity?

She races up the hill for her brother and sees the men leaping out of their trucks. Trucks that judging by the bent door and busted headlight had hit each other. Trucks that had hit each other and hit Lorne and sent him wheeling out of control onto the road where he is lying now, clinging to his leg and whimpering.

Julie shouts, "Let me see," surprised by the ferocity in her voice. Lorne is holding tight, both hands around his thigh, squeezing and looking up at the sky, breathing through his teeth. Blood leaking between his fingers and Julie wanting to retch but knowing she has to see more. She asks is it broken and he shakes his head and then she asks if he's okay. He nods and she hugs him and says "Lorne you have to let me see" and without warning he pulls his hands back and she beholds the bare pink flesh of his thigh, like the inside of a lobster tail. A veiny ropework of ligaments thatched with a snaggle of sinew. The scared hiss of her brother's breath and the naked muscle twitching as he squirms.

Then a crimson pool fills the wound. Turns the seam near-black before bubbling and leaking and spilling over onto the pavement. Her brother's blood running fast down his leg and she pulls off her T-shirt and ties it tight around the lacerated limb. Lorne on his back and his face is white, almost clear, as he drifts away from her. She takes his head in her hands and rubs his forehead, saying "Lorne! Lorne!" and crying out for water.

Julie has seen the blood and she has seen her brother's bare flesh—his thigh muscle pink and twitching like a tongue. She has seen the flesh beneath that veil of skin and now, as a man splashes water on Lorne and he comes to, as she helps him rise to his feet and clamber dazed into the man's pickup, she knows that she can never unsee this thing. That some part of her will always see her brother's body as a writhing amalgam of vein and bone, a fragile marriage of blood and flesh.

The ceiling fan in the Clinton motel turns slowly overhead and she finds herself thankful for this small stability. Thankful as she lies awake with no hope of sleeping. Lies awake thinking of her brother. Their childhood homes in Vancouver, Sarnia, Boston, and finally Halifax. Her brother at five, his face covered in Easter chocolate. Her brother holding vigil in her bedroom after she'd been traumatized by *The Exorcist*. Her brother bringing her sliced grapefruit when she was sick with strep throat. Her brother racing by her on the ski hill, dragging his poles between his legs so that the snow flew up in her face. A flash of rage and resentment and then, when he glanced back beaming over his shoulder, a contagion of joy.

She rises at three in the morning and walks out onto the patio overlooking the parking lot. A cold night in early

May and the air wet with North Atlantic breeze. She has wrapped herself in a coarse motel blanket but still she finds herself shivering.

Franz appears on the patio and she thinks who is this man? This tall and generous man from Senegal who had wooed her, once, with lines by Damas and Césaire, lines by Léopold Sédar Senghor, lines with a concave lilt that were sublime perhaps because they eluded understanding as much in English as in French. This man who just the night before had crawled into bed reciting Baudelaire—*Viens, mon beau chat, sur mon coeur amoureux; / Retiens les griffes de ta patte.*

This man with his serpent sun, his vampire flowers. This man who could look at the sky and see patterns where she had always seen a senseless slur of cloud and chaos. Who points upwards, now, and says that that star glowing rose is Mars. This man trying to comfort her with a discourse about the god of war and the difference between Homer and Virgil until she says no, stop. Until she says Mars is a planet where nothing can breathe and regrets saying so as the sadness spills through his dark eyes. She says maybe she just needs to be alone right now and he nods gently, kisses the back of her head, and slips back inside through the patio door. She looks up at Mars and imagines her brother there, alone, as the storms build and close in on that sapphire world. She sees him standing alone on that uninhabited planet, staring out into the vast indifferent open of space. And she sees the clouds drawing closer and closer, her brother helpless against them. Whether on Mars or lodged in a coal seam in East Rock, Nova Scotia, her brother is alone. Alone in a world that is closing in around him and there is nothing she can do.

After falling into a fitful sleep, she dreams an avalanche. It is a spring day and they are traversing, trying to get to a chute on the far side of a bowl. They are in the middle of a wide alpine tongue when the slope cracks and the white world buckles beneath them—buckles and roars and begins to slide.

She looks for Franz and can't see him and there is nothing to do but cling on as one ski comes off and the white overcomes her and she is looking for blue, scanning for sky, finding nothing but a flailing chuck of white. Trying to swim to stay on top but bottom and top slur together and there is no ground, now, no ground or sky. Everything a blast of gravity, sucking her onward, blind and helpless and nothing to do but give in. The world slanted and rushing as she tosses her limbs in a parody of breaststroke and feels the snow begin to settle, begin to clamp.

Which is when she remembers to put her hands in front of her face. She knows enough to raise her arms and put her gloves in front of her mouth as the snow congeals—a quicksand abruptly frozen. Her head a thunder of pulse and echo and wheezing breath. The profound silence of the outside world and her body a deafening clamour. Her breath is panicked and she tells herself to settle, wills herself to wait. She counts her breaths and tries not to think about how many she has left.

Gradually, the panic eases. There is nothing left to do but breathe and wait. She is cold, cold and drifting into an eerily pleasant calm. The snow around her seems soft, now, as she floats through time, her body a cloud bathed in moonlight.

In the nineteenth century, horses from Sable Island were regularly captured and taken to work in the Cape Breton mines, hauling tubs of coal through the dinge of the underground railways. Horses raised feral, chewing marram in the salt-harsh air of the open Atlantic, would surface once a year for the colliery holiday. If they were fortunate their stables would be near the shaft, where now and then a breeze licked through.

She wakes to the sound of the radio and rises fast in bed. Franz is saying "I thought you would want to" and she says "yes, yes, of course." The boys sit bleary on the couch and when she looks at them they are plaintive, hungry for consolation. On the radio they are saying "fifteen," saying "recovered," saying "bodies." The reporter on the radio is saying that fifteen men have been found dead and the "rescue effort" has officially become a "recovery effort." They are asking family members to come identify bodies and she is thinking *no*, thinking *of course not*, knowing that she will go, must go.

She stands beside her brother at the hospital as the red-haired doctor stoops over him. Their mother is rushing over and their father is at a meeting at the plant and cannot be reached. So it is just the two of them as the nurse cleans the wound and the doctor prepares his tools. The doctor asks what their father does for a living and when Lorne answers he puts the long needle into the thigh. Lorne winces and clings to Julie's hand. The doctor injects more anaesthetic and the nurse asks what school does Lorne go to, says she knows a teacher there. The doctor asks, "Can you feel this?" Lorne shakes his head and the nurse wipes some blood and then the first stitch goes through. There is a piece of wax paper over the wound so Lorne cannot see and he asks Julie what it looks like. She tells him that it is strange, how thick the skin is, how easy the stitch runs through. "No," he says, "I mean on the inside." And so she tells him, as the doctor runs the thread through his flesh, about the red like lava, twitching beneath the blood. She tells her little brother a story about the lean muscle in him, like a giant tongue streaked with strands of fat. He holds her hand and the doctor finishes and he says he's sad he will never get to see it, will never know what his body looks like on the inside.

Where was he now, her balding blue-eyed brother? Her brother who had moved with her from town to town as their father designed refineries for Streamline Energy. Her brother who'd sat in the garage night after night, making go-karts out of old baby strollers. Her brother with a scar on his palm from when he'd cut himself changing an oil filter, that thick black grease seeping in and staining him under the skin. The boy who had flunked and stumbled through high school, who'd become a navy seaman and an Alberta pipefitter and been so happy, that September, to come back to Nova Scotia. Her brother whose quadriceps she'd seen twitching beneath skin drawn back like a lip. Not yet thirty and now he was buried underground in a seam of earth that had raged and rumbled and closed.

Franz ushers the boys into the Camry and they begin the drive from Clinton to East Rock. As they cruise the two-lane country road she thinks of the seam sprawling beneath them. She thinks of the coal limning those caverns like some dark and precious blood clotted in the underground.

They arrive at the makeshift hockey rink morgue and Julie thinks of the fissure beneath her, the ribs of the drift sloughing chunks of gaseous rock. She thinks of the methane blooming in those earthly arteries and wants to blame the gas, longs to blame the methane. But she finds herself unable. How can she fault that gas for wanting to escape its earthen womb, to crawl out into the open and ride the sky?

Franz stays in the car with the boys as she enters the rink, inhales the sour chemical reek of Zamboni and formaldehyde. She gives her name to the attendant and walks slowly across the carpeted ice. Families huddle and whisper and she feels herself move through them, a finger passing through candle flame.

Six months before, Julie had stood with her brother and her sons on the Halifax waterfront. Lorne was down for

Thanksgiving. They watched a grey sky slide over a grey ocean and Lorne talked about benefits, talked about down payments, about a semi-detached in New Glasgow. He said maybe a couple children of his own. Jack was sprinting up the huge concrete wave over and over and never making it to the top, sliding down each time on his corduroyed knees. Owen stood riveted by the three candy-cane smokestacks rising up from Dartmouth until Lorne told him it was called Tufts Cove Generating Station. It was built on the site of the Mi'kmaq gathering place that was obliterated by the *Imo*, the place where Jerry Lonecloud took a jettisoned screw through the eye and staggered half-blind about the wreckage, screaming for the two daughters he would never find.

"Haven't you ever heard of the Halifax Explosion?"

Owen said he had but not that part. Lorne pointed out towards the Eastern Shore where there was a little colony of smokestacks and scaffolding and concrete stills the size of houses, lights blinking on like a tired, tangled Christmas. Lorne asked Owen if he knew what that was and the boy said no. "It's called a refinery," Lorne said. "Your grandfather, he helped build that." Owen looked up at him like he was confused at the connection between his grandfather and this dazzle of ugliness. "You know," Lorne said, and he no longer seemed to be talking to his nephew, "most people go their whole lives walking past refineries and they never even notice them, never even see the vats of crude being processed."

Jack came to wrangle Owen and the two of them scampered away to play pirates in a creaky, salt-rotten ship with frayed nets of rope luffing off the sides. Half-watching her children, Julie asked her brother how he could choose to go work underground. First he said it wasn't that different from what she did, wasn't much more dangerous than flying for a living, soaring through the sky in a pressurized cabin offering cookies or pretzels as if salt or sugar could assuage the everyday hubris of a passenger jet.

He took a moment staring out at the slate-grey harbour then answered again. This time he said that he wanted to go below, wanted to open up the earth and touch what was inside. He knew it was strange but sometimes he felt like a beetle or a mole and he just wanted to bore right down into the darkness and let it hold him.

"Why do you think people like to be buried down there?" She must have seemed frightened because he looked at her and added, "Course it's not so bad coming back up at the end of the day."

Julie moves from table to table, surveys the body bags with their yellow labels, many still blank. She approaches each figure, scans the palms for that familiar rind of oil, looks deep into every face. Faces wiped clean but forever dark from the blackness that claimed them. Men in their twenties and thirties, cheeks still puffed with boyhood bloat. Men with thick moustaches and deep smile lines. Men who'd worn plaid, who'd sat in blinds and waited for bucks to saunter out into clearings. Men who'd held guitars and pool cues, told jokes and stories, tickled babies and watched time buckle and drift in the eyes of their children.

She treads the ice among this maze of bodies and feels herself a failed Antigone. Here in a hockey rink surrounded by the unknown dead Julie realizes that she needs a body. She had not expected this feeling, has never felt it before. Until this point she had wanted to find him alive but now she feels a new longing emerge, a longing for her brother's corpse.

And then she sees it. Not here in this crude crypt rimmed with ads for Sobeys, for St. FX, for Courtney Clarence attorney at law. She sees her brother as he is, as he will remain— caught in the slough and the rock, a slash of coal across his temple, a boulder squatting on his blasted lungs. She sees Lorne crushed and motionless in the indifferent dark. Sees him inert and pale and filthy, cradled by the world he had been compelled to explore. Sees his eyes, open and peering through the darkness, staring at the roof of the drift, his eyes locked in stunned wonder. The strange thing is that he looks tranquil, clutched in that petrified seam. Her brother looks serene as he stares into the rock, finding patterns only he will ever know in that darkling, vascular world. The earth holding her brother close and him feeling the safe, steady grip of the rocks, their unwavering contain.

Around 5:20 in the morning on May 9th, 1992, a worker using a continuous miner to cut into the Foord Coal Seam hit a strand of pyrite braided into the coal vein. The pyrite produced sparks, causing a draft of methane to ignite. Gaining momentum instantly, the flaming gas roared through the chambers of the mine, setting off a series of rockfalls and explosions, collapsing the roof and replacing all oxygen with poisonous carbon monoxide. The fifteen workers whose bodies were recovered are presumed to have died in less than a minute. The ten men whose bodies were never found were working in a vulnerable part of the mine where the post-explosion rockslides were particularly aggressive. These men are thought to have died instantly.

The Streamline Energy Corporation will act predictably. A parade of clones will say "standard procedure," say "protocol," say "safety regulations." The surviving miners will have to wait six years to receive twelve weeks' severance.

The memory of her brother will burrow inside Julie, boring gradually deeper. His emptiness will eventually settle in her right side, between the seventh and eighth ribs. Sometimes—walking along the waterfront with her son, standing up from the toilet, clearing a miniature wine bottle from a tray table as turbulence picks up—she will feel a gentle burn in that spot, like the cool kiss of VapoRub. And at this point there will be almost nothing so dear to her as this strange soft hurt, this cherished cleft of pain.

Shortly after her brother's funeral, Julie will begin to have the dream. In the dream there is nothing but total blackness, but it is a blackness that sings, a blackness that hums. In the dream she reaches out and touches the walls and they are chalky, gritty on her fingers and knuckles and palms and she feels each crook and rise like a dark bathymetry, like a dead language coming back to life. "Most people look at a rock and they see a rock," Lorne had said to her once. "Me I see stories. I see coal and coke, I see sediments and cystics, anticlines and binders and pyrites."

He had said this and she sees it now but she doesn't tell him that, doesn't whisper to him. In the dream they don't talk and they don't need to. They lie still in the total darkness, at rest, at last, in the drift.

HOW YOUR LIFE

This is how your life has been lately: you go for an evening jog because your body has become a cellulite farm on account of binge drinking and late-night poutine and no word of a lie an owl swoops down and clutches your head. As if the whole lung-burning, tit-lurching experience wasn't enough without some yellow-eyed demon descending out of the full moon as you're huffing through Point Pleasant. You're listening to Katy so you don't hear a thing and then there are claws in your head and a nursing home smell and something is trying to fly away with your skull. You're swatting your head and hitting feathers and talons and the deranged animal which is probably rabid starts flapping and making weird bird noises that are not scary-cute Halloween hoos until finally you collapse on the ground and rip off one of your shoes and start going batshit. Your peripherals catch someone rushing to your rescue and you think no it can't be and then yes of course it's the hot butcher from the market and you're thinking, *that's right I am swinging a sneaker at my own head right now.*

There's a crunching noise and a burn worse than a bikini wax and when you look up an enormous owl is flying away holding a ribboning clump of your hair. The hair you spent 200 dollars on yesterday. The hair that causes strangers to ask "where are you from?" and mean "I'm having trouble placing you racially."

You do not finish your run. You do not accept the hot butcher's entreaties to help but instead slink away crying/gasping. You go home and call animal control and the generic dad-voice on the other end tells you that yeah, there have been a lot of owls behaving weirdly in the city lately and they've had a couple of similar reports. No, the animal is not rabid. It is quite sane—the bounding ponytail of the harmless, new-leaf-overturning jogger simply appears to the hungry owl eye as a delicious scurrying rodent.

You do not run again that entire week despite your May resolution. And in fact there is a pathetically large part of you that feels secretly happy that you now basically have an excuse not to run again for your entire life. Instead of jogging, you do Pogue and Lower Deck and Alehouse with more than your usual gusto. One night you're stumbling down Barrington with a dude named Blane, telling him you can't believe you swiped right in spite of the fact that his name was Blane, when you step on a syringe that's lying on the sidewalk. There's a sound like biting last year's candy-cane and when you look down there's a tiny disgusting sidewalk needle next to an archipelago of broken glass. You are wearing flats and you don't know if there are microscopic cuts on your feet but you're thinking probably and you're thinking Ebola thinking HIV thinking when was the last time you got tested anyway and you collapse on the curb and start to cry/gasp. When you look up Blane is gone and it's almost definitely for the best although you were pretty excited to text Miranda that you'd let a guy with dreadlocks and an idiotic name like Blane into your bed. Miranda loves that shit because she's got sexual claustrophobia from sleeping with Luke and only Luke and now that she's eleventy months pregnant she can barely get off her chair so she probably/hopefully has not had sex in a few weeks. You think about calling Miranda to cry/gasp into her ear but then you think she's probably asleep or giving birth or sitting on the toilet all night because it's easier than getting up sixteen times to pee. It's too late to call your mother and you definitely would not let her hear you cry/gasp anyway so you go home, fry some dumplings, and fall asleep watching *Pride and Prejudice*.

Are you really over school? Are you really going to start your own organic dairy farm/artisanal cheese shop with a sign that reads "shoppe" just so you can upstage your new archnemesis the hot butcher by opening a stand in the same mall where you and he now work and showing generous cleave and outselling him? You have just received letters of acceptance with decent funding from grad schools in Edmonton and Ottawa, though you'd never heard of a master's in public health before Dr. Pottie started pushing it when you met for coffee in September. You are not sure you can leave this place again, not sure you even want to move forward. You want to remain twenty-six living in this place you love and not committing to any of the various futures that could ruin or wrack or age you. You remember when you were seven and Miranda was nine you stood in the backyard watching inchworms crawl along your chipped white fence. She asked about who you would want to marry when you grew up and you said no one because you didn't want to grow up, seven was the perfect age. You wanted to stay seven forever and you still do.

Your parents have been pushing the master's although your dentist father's still on about upgrading and med school and you have to admit you like the idea of being better than your bilingual government employee sister at one thing ever. Your parents are in favour of grad school or med school or dental school or law school but they are definitely not pro cheese shoppe. You yourself remain baffled as to why Dr. Pottie and other experts are remotely excited about your undergrad thesis on urban versus rural sexual habits. You'd only picked the subject because it seemed pretty obvious that country folk would spread more STIs than urbanites. Your logic: fewer potential partners plus less to do equals lots of partner trading within small social pool. According to Kinsey's largely discredited but still compelling research, fifty percent of rural males have had a sexual encounter with an animal. So there's that. Then there's incest. You once heard that people in Newfoundland developed an app that would tell them how much genetic material they shared with the person they were meeting. First dates started by opening this app and bumping iPhones. You remember thinking this was genius but also terrifying, bumping iPhones being basically the new sex anyway. You wonder what're the chances that the hot butcher is related to you. Then, sicker, you think maybe that's *why* you find him dangerously desirable. You remember watching a documentary where an Australian father had left his family when the kids were babies and then picked up a young blonde twenty years later and found himself in a toxically spectacular sexual relationship with his biological daughter. "She's beautiful," he said in his Crocodile Dundee accent. "I made her and she's beautiful." There used to be a girl at the grocery store from Cape Breton and one time she got drunk and told you that as a teenager she'd slept with two of her cousins before she even found out they were her cousins. Is this research or gossip? According to Dr. Pottie, it's research. Any case for a while it seemed like a master's was a good idea but then you came to think you were only doing school to postpone real life.

You spend the morning taking Facebook quizzes and telling yourself you won't post the results and then posting the results. Then you go to work and as you're weighing portions of water buffalo Havarti your new archnemesis the hot butcher comes up to the counter. He says "Hey" and you say "Yo" and panic about your hair patch-up job as you pretend to be really focused on weighing your one hundred millionth portion of buff waterlow.

"Hey," he says again. "Callie?"

How does this cleaver-wielding meatman know your name?

He grins and nods at your chest. Your nametag. "Yep, that's me."

"Ferdinand," he says sincerely, and you are struggling not to laugh in his face and then realizing maybe the ridiculous name will keep some of the other girls away as he reaches out to shake your hand. You have never found a hand sexy before, but his is perfect. Hairless and muscular. Long, shapely fingers. The fingers of an artist.

So his hand is just dangling there until you show him you're wearing latex gloves and currently handling a large hunk of cheese and he smiles, embarrassed. You look down at the cheese. For the first time ever it looks exciting—porous and liquid and full of thrill and energy.

"Are you okay? That was pretty insane, what happened yesterday. I saw the whole thing." You tell him yeah, you set a deadly pace up those hills. He snorts. If his eyes were blue they would twinkle. "No, I mean with the owl. Was it an owl?"

"Yeah, yeah." You shrug, adjust your latex gloves. "That's just my pet owl, Ariel."

Though you're expecting the sexiest laugh ever, in fact his laugh sounds a bit like the pigs from *Hannibal.* "You're hilarious," he says. "Like from *The Little Mermaid?*"

"Sure. Need any cheese?"

"No, actually. I'm vegan."

"A vegan butcher?"

He grins.

"Hilarious," you say, thinking *please don't laugh again*. He laughs again and it's less bad this time. You're guessing the first one was just his nervous laugh then you're thinking if he's nervous that's probably a good sign.

He swallows. You bag some cheese. He swallows again then blurts: "Want to go for a walk sometime?"

A walk. Does it involve alcohol? "Does it involve owls?"

He smiles like a triumphant grandfather clutching a fat trout. "It can," he says, keying the pin into his iPhone.

Family dinner on the dark side. Despite your mother's panic—her eldest daughter is thirty-six weeks along and set to unload a tiny human at the most minute provocation—Miranda came down from Ottawa for an impromptu visit. She's been on mat leave for two weeks and it's already razing her patience and besides you and your sister always enjoy an excuse to return to the nest. Although you moved to Halifax when you were nineteen, going back across the bridge for dinners and kitchen raids is in you like salt in ocean air.

"I don't feel anything. Isn't it supposed to like kick or dance or light a cigarette in there?"

You're sitting on the faded maroon living room couch, the upholstery shredded by cats long dead, with one hand on your sister's swollen gut. She's lifted her pregnancy pants to reveal a bruise-dark navel the size of an Olympic medal, wreathed with scraggled tentacles of vein.

"Yeah, sometimes. Once I actually saw the full hand, all five fingers prodding through my gutflesh like it was trying to mark a cave wall. But mostly it's supposed to sleep."

"Sounds nice."

"Do you want one?"

"What?"

"A kid. Not now, but someday?"

You remember when you were a child you had two female cats, neither of them neutered. Lou never got pregnant but Sabotage was a kitten factory. Five a year, every summer. Every year your mother would sigh "Jesus not again" and your father would joke that he was going to drown them in Lake Banook but really all of you loved building nests in cardboard boxes and naming them Fatty and Runty and watching them play and learn, nurse and grow. Even your father made a point of building a whelping box and saying the words "whelping box" whenever possible. You remember how slimy the kittens looked when they were born, the rank uterine film Sabotage had to lick off. But mostly what you remember is Lou taking that tabby in her mouth and bringing it to her own nest in the closet, trying to nurse it with her milkless teats. Stunned by that strange parody of motherhood, you had longed to see Lou birth a tiny squinting kitten of her own. Pined to see her curl down to lick her own child's amniotic sac, tonguing that membrane until the great rushing world spilled through.

"A kid? I don't know. Does the kid want me?"

"Don't do that. You always do that."

"What?"

"Conceal yourself. You need to let people in."

"Woah," you say, raising palms. "Fine," you say, and you tell her about Lou and the tabby kitten and that day in the backyard and how you still want to be seven forever. But you are also reluctantly thinking that maybe she's right, maybe you have a habit of concealing yourself from yourself.

Miranda says sad about the cat but that is not you and you sit there for a while in silence, listening to the sound of your mother tenderly cursing at a béchamel. Finally Miranda starts telling you about how her husband's septuagenarian parents are trying to get her to baptize her baby and it is nice to laugh. Miranda is not even remotely smug about her pregnancy even though she's more the platinum child than ever and even though her husband Luke is miraculously both super intelligent and mega dad-hot. For the longest time you tried not to admit it to yourself but now you feel better if you just concede that he's a dorky fox. The kind of guy who takes off his thick glasses to display shimmering crystal blues and then reveals smooth hairless pecs underneath his dad-plaid. The worst/best part about Miranda is she's so sweet she doesn't notice that it might be hard for you to be the adopted girl in a family full of beaming blond superstars. And the other worst/best part about your older sister is that in spite of living a predictable/hateable yuppie life including a golf club membership and a purebred Australian shepherd and a mortgage, she is still genuinely fun.

"It's my fucking baby so go fuck yourself," she is saying now, imagining that she is speaking to Luke's insanely fit parents who are late seventies and threatening to live forever. "All these people making demands about this fucking baby before it's even tasted air. No I haven't picked a name. No I don't want to know the sex. No I don't want to get my kid baptized because no I'm not already thinking about its death and what it might say to Saint Peter and I don't believe in Peter anyway. I'm going to have a baby and I'm terrified of the whole hospital part and I'm still not sure this was even a good idea so everyone can fuck off. It's my fucking baby so go fuck yourself," she is saying, and you are laughing, laughing as your father arrives home from the office and your mother sings dinner's ready and you feel grateful to Miranda because you feel she has bared herself, that you are trusted and sober and home.

You have dinner and there's wine and it's pleasant and afterwards you're in the living room having chamomile tea when you see your sister's stomach lurch. She is leaning back in an armchair, two hands on her veiny watermelon, and something buckles in that melon, the movement visible right through her shirt. It's like that scene in *Aliens*, like a misplaced heart thumping in her gut. But then your sister coos and lifts her shirt and rolls her weird pants down, and then she invites you to touch and talk to the fetus and you feel your heart grow and jolt and almost pur. Your father thuds over and puts his hand there too and your mother rushes in from the kitchen and finally you understand. Some part of you has always imagined you'd have children one day but whenever you've thought realistically about the vaginal tears and the foul, spontaneous farting and the stretched bits and the word "perineum" you could never quite come to terms with the idea of actually choosing to accept this burden. Now you begin to get it. You are touching Miranda's belly and her nameless, genderless child is thudding through her flesh into your hand, saying *hello*, saying *auntie*, saying *help me I'm alive*.

Wednesday morning—probably because your ambulatory non-alcoholic date is the following evening—you get the trauma pruned out of your hair then spend several hours berating yourself in front of a mirror until you go for a run. But because of the whole demonic-avian-descending-from-the-heavens incident, you take your pre-date run at the Human Body Refinement Factory even though you've sworn you'd never go back to the Human Body Refinement Factory ever since your Sensation and Perception prof accosted you on the new "curve" treadmill.

"Callie!" he shouted, coming right up and leaning on the left handlebar. You could see the guy on the climbing wall looking over, wondering about this stooping greyhair. "I haven't seen you since your final assignment and I just wanted to say how truly excellent your reading of intragender versus intergender eye contact was and I thought it was appropriate to say so as you were sweating and gasping in one of your occasional manic attempts to reduce your love handle and/

or thigh size even though every time you lose five pounds it seems to come directly off the boobs or the parts of the butt you actually like. I'm sure you realize that going stupid-hard until you feel the sour breath of the reaper does not make up for sporadic and irregular gym exercise but hey power to you."

Anyway those were not his exact words but close enough and that was only the beginning and you ended your workout early just to avoid this gaunt and overly gym-talkative professor and now you are pretty sure that you will see him as you scan the Human Body Refinement Factory, stepping onto the treadmill. But of course it is not the creepshow professor you see but Ferdinand himself and you are already crouch-walking directly back to the change room when he sees you and flashes his huge white smile and starts walking towards you, neck muscles taut and glistening with a brine of sweat.

You say hi, terrified, still scanning the gym though you don't know who for and he says a few things you pay no attention to. At one point he looks like he wants you to laugh so you giggle but then you start coughing and mutter some lame goodbye and he asks if you're still on for tomorrow night and you shrug for some reason but then manage to say yes of course and he says he'll text you. Then you are downstairs in the bathroom staring at yourself in the mirror for a long time and you are amazed but still not happy that despite everything he still seems to find you attractive. You drink water. You wait it out. Girls with taut, waxed bodies come down and shower and look at you like "why are your nipples so large?" and leave. A women's volleyball team passes through. He must be gone by now and you are trying to decide whether to go up and finish your workout after all but by this point you are deliriously hungry because you never eat for a few hours before a workout or you'll throw up after three strides. So here you are on the bench in the gym locker room, an enormous megastill emptiness.

"Is his name actually Ferdinand?" Miranda's driving you home from dinner and asking about the butcher and you've already disclosed far too much so you remain silent and hope she will take a hint and change subjects. As she pulls onto the McDonald Bridge you look down over the city lights and think how much you love this place—the preposterous hills and lethargic public transportation, the meandering, narrow streets, the bright colours of the wooden houses on Agricola, the ones locals call "the three sisters" although you've always seen four. Mostly, though, you love the oldness of it all. This is what you noticed when you came back from Calgary to finish your degree after things went sour with your ex. You noticed the long vowels in the words "tahl" and "bahr" and "hahrbour," you noticed and were suddenly fond of Georgian buildings and the town clock. Also you became conscious of the fog. The way it whisked, spectral, across the midnight streets. How it shrouded the moon. Its thickness, wheeling through the salt summer air. The way it hung around the streetlamps, glossing the city in hard-boiled glow. The way you would go for a walk and find that, though there hadn't been a single raindrop, your clothes were soaked when you reached home. The fog in this place loosed something ancient in you, some millennia of beauty.

You are looking out over the lights glittering off the still, black harbour, looking past the hooked suicide fence and thinking, as you've often thought, what it would be like to jump off the bridge, to enter the wet blackness below. Though the news doesn't usually report it, many people have jumped from this bridge over the years. And though the water doesn't seem that far away, most of them have died. You do not think this in a suicidal way—that is, you do not actually consider jumping. It is a harmless curiosity. What actually happens to the body when it hits the water? You have heard that unlucky people sometimes survive the one hundred-plus metre fall.

That in order to ensure death you have to land horizontal, like a bellyflop. But you like the idea of diving, launching a flawless swan dive and soaring gracefully, gracefully, before splitting the water like a well-placed axe sinking into a log. You like the idea of shredding through the night air towards the gold-speckled blackness below, of parting the ocean and searing straight down towards the harbour floor. Of simply vanishing, there, in the bottom. Of entering something deeper than you.

From the peak of the bridge, Miranda utters the old cliché: "The best part about Dartmouth is the view of Halifax."

"True enough," you say, thinking that there really is some truth to the saying. Thinking that you love Dartmouth too and wondering if the wisdom of the line is that the best part about any place is the shadow of someplace else.

"Ever think about moving back here?" you ask your sister as the car clears the peak and begins to descend.

"Of course. I'd love to come home one day. Things would have to be right though."

"You mean jobs?"

"Yeah, no jobs here. No good ones anyway. But not just that. You know moving to Ottawa was the best thing I ever did."

"Sure: husband, mortgage, baby. None of that here."

She pauses, thoughtful. Takes a breath. "When I was living here after my degree, time seemed to stop. Years of idling. Couldn't get it together to go back to school. Applying for 'real' jobs every day and making minimum plus pennies at the coffee shop. Couldn't meet anyone exciting because I knew everyone already. I stayed because I love the place and I'd still rather be here than Ottawa. But I'd rather be me in Ottawa than me here. It's weird. If you love a place, you've got to leave it. I don't know."

You say no, you get it. And you have never been sure what that "it" means but you are sure you get something.

Date night arrives. You and Ferdinand actually go for a walk across the Commons and down to the public gardens and you are wondering what's up with his enormous man purse until he pulls a blanket out and lays it on the ground. You sit down and he produces a bottle of pinot noir and some baguette and Comté and a sausage joke comes but you stifle it and just sit there cultivating cuteness. How does one sit on a blanket in a park? You try triangle, then up-dog, settle for cross-legged. The Comté has a perfect sweat going but you're trying to peck at it because you don't want him to know the walk drained your fragile resources and your calves are still burning from yesterday's treadmill refinement process. The wine gets him talking and surprise surprise he knows the name of every bird and tree in the park and he does a little yoga and grows his own tomatoes and if you wanted to go with him sometime he'd love to show you the treehouse he built in the woods near Fall River when he was twelve years old.

A bit more wine and you start leaking verbal and yes you are telling him about your ancestor who was hanged as a witch. Well, not really technically your ancestor, being that you are adopted and the only visible minority in your family and all you know about your birth mother is that she came to Dartmouth from Turks and Caicos and she no longer lives anywhere close. But you don't tell the Ferdster about all that. Not yet. You can put that suitcase in the baggage check for at least a week or two. You tell about Mary Easty.

Your mother has told you the story eight thousand times and you have never tired of hearing it. How Mary Easty gave one of the most articulate denials of witchery heard at the Salem trials but Judge Hathorne imprisoned her anyway. Your mother says Hathorne must have had a thing for little girls, a grown man buying into all that fairy dust. She says how Mary was briefly and mysteriously released from jail for a few days, how she wrote a petition asking for fair trial, how she refused to confess, how she missed the first round but hanged, finally, on September 22nd, 1692. Your mother says Mary Easty died because she spoke the language of the law, not the language of witchcraft and delusional little girls. It was an honourable death but every time your mother tells the story you imagine the pillory and the scowling deep-voiced judges and you know that if you were there you would confess. You would make up wild accusations and dive onto the floor in phony paroxysms and do whatever it took to make Abigail Williams your new best friend. You know this because you know you are weak and selfish at the core but also because you love, sometimes, to let your imagination roam wild and dangerous. Because you know that there was some large and real part of Abigail that really believed she was being tortured by witches. That that night in the woods making brew with Tituba she had really seen a man with the feet of an ungulate, really seen Sarah Good pealing through the night sky, that she had been moved by those things and wanted to live in that dreamworld of devils and witchery far more than the world of pious books and obedient silence and the hard oak pews of the town church.

Ferdinand is listening eagerly and eventually he says yeah witches are pretty cool and asks if you ever saw *The Witches of Eastwick*. You say yes and agree to watch it sometime, thinking about legs rubbing under blankets. After the wine is finished the two of you watch the sun begin to set. You inch closer and lick your lips but there's no lean-in. The butcher's tongue does not make an appearance and when you think of it that way you're a little relieved. You're thinking maybe he's not interested but then you remember about the wine and baguette and Comté and really who acts that smooth when initiating a platonic hetero friendship? Some uniformed gnomes come around and start locking things and Ferdinand rolls up his blanket and shoves it in his man-sack and says you should come back to his place because there's something he wants to show you. He seems nervous, saying it, and you want to ease the awkward so you make a crack about tenderloin. He laughs and says no not that and you head out together towards South Park Street. When he hails a cab and says "Gottingen and Charles" you feel relieved that he lives in your neighbourhood and there will be no more pilgrimage this evening.

The damp grassy smell of the Commons pours in through the taxi window and Ferdinand puts his hand on your leg and you let him keep it there even though you're thinking he really should kiss before making proprietary semi-committal gestures. The cab passes the chic coffee shops and the microbrews and he asks if you remember when Gottingen was the ghetto and you say no you spent most of your childhood in Dartmouth. He laughs and says I guess that's better than Fall River.

"The best part of Dartmouth is the view of Halifax." You say the line wistfully, hoping to give it new meaning as you watch a string of taillights arc over the McKay.

"Is the best part of Halifax the view of Toronto?"

"Nova Scotians can't see past Moncton."

He laughs, asks what you mean. You say the usual. You say about unemployment and alcoholism and the fisheries and welfare. You say everyone you know who has something resembling a "career" had to leave the province to get it. You tell him about your ex and his friends, all flying to Alberta to work the oil patch, how it's fine when you're twenty-one but what happens when you're thirty and want to start a family and you can never stay home more than three weeks at a stretch, if you've been lucky enough to make it to thirty without a meth habit. You say how you're twenty-six and started undergrad late and have no idea what comes next because most of your friends with degrees are serving tables or working retail or learning trades and have never left the province.

You say how there's some sick compulsion about this peninsula. You say the water level's rising and we're all going to drown here clinging to fiddles and slabs of distressed barnwood. You admit that you don't want to leave either, which makes you sad because the way you see it the people around you are split into two groups: those who leave and flourish and those who stay and squander.

"I don't see it like that," he says. "I'm here, I'm happy. I got a degree and now I'm doing my own thing, butchering. I own the business. Nothing fancy but I'm comfortable, happy."

"Happy butchering!" You announce it like a wedding toast, then laugh way too loud. You think you may have ruined date night, but you also feel that you have never heard anyone say something so honest and brave. So you hope you have not ruined date night.

Ferdinand's loft is littered with milk crates full of vinyls and stacks of second hand books and walls covered in sepia photos you truly hope he didn't develop himself. Yes, there is a ukulele and a banjo. He takes your wrist and leads you into the bedroom and you're expecting to see a sex swing or at least a set of handcuffs but instead he pulls you into the closet and you're looking at a diminutive calico princess with three blobs of furry adorability nursing on her sagging teats. You sit down and just watch the animals for a long time before you're bold enough to pet them. The mother doesn't seem to mind so when the kittens are done nursing you rub a little black one until it lolls over and lets you stroke its belly. Then Ferdinand hands you a white fluffy one with an orange tail and says, "This one's yours if you want. I call her 'Ariel.'"

"Ariel," you repeat. You take her between two hands and she looks at you and her eyes are green all the way through. No white at all. You have seen so many cats in your life and never been so astonished by this radiant lack of white. Ariel play-bites your thumb and you stroke her unfairly soft mane, then move to the neck, your whole life diluting in the ocean of her purr.

Ferdinand goes into the living room shouting "Robert Johnson" and puts on a scratchy old blues vinyl. You set Ariel down and crawl softly into the bed, peeling your clothes off quietly and preparing to surprise him, thinking what better time than now to take a risk?

When you were nine you became fixated on Sable Island. Your mother bought books and you learned about the heavy fog and the jackknife currents that had caused hundreds of ships to wreck on this improbable crescent of sand. You learned about the *Delight*, the *Manhasset*, and the *Merrimac*. You learned about the grey seals that breed each summer on the island's beaches but mostly you were transfixed by the horses, the more than 500 wild horses that may have descended from confiscated Acadian stock but no one quite knows where they came from or how they got there. You liked to think that a few of them had survived one of the shipwrecks and afterwards they'd bred and thrived for centuries. You did not like to think about the horses the Cape Breton coal mines took to work underground. What you liked was imagining the horses running in the open air, galloping full speed over the island's forty-kilometre stretch. The island so long and narrow and free of predators and it seemed to be built for a horse to roam and sprint, to fly over the soft wet sand. Your mother once saw you staring transfixed at a picture of a feral horse thundering over the beach and she asked if you wanted a horse of your own, if you might like to try riding. You had to think about it but finally you decided that what you liked was the idea of a horse running riderless through the open. You told your mother that you did not want to own a horse—you wanted to be one.

Ariel and Ferdinand, Ferdinand and Ariel. These two have entered your life and that life has become pink and effervescent. Life has become champagne or at least sparkling white. Yes the sex has been better than good and there have been choice cuts of premium, hormone-free, grass-fed. Yes Ferd barbeques a ravishing lamb burger and yes you feel that some combination of regular intimacy and living with an adorable calico kitten has considerably alleviated your anxieties about how you have to let U of A know by the end of the week. No you have not answered Dr. Chen from Carleton's email saying you could have another month to decide and they would like to give you more money but you have been going for regular outdoor jogs with minimal owl phobia and boozing less and you've kind of quit Tinder. You are thinking sure. Sure you could settle in Halifax and start an organic dairy business and buy a modest home and live with your butcher and have beautiful mixed babies with his hazel eyes and his strong chin and his knowledge of wine. Yes Miranda returned to Ottawa and gave birth to a baby boy and chose to name him Jed. You find it strange how Jed is the only thing Miranda can talk about on the phone now—bragging about how at three weeks he can hold his head up with his own strength, bragging about the way he air-punches with his fat little arms, bragging about the strength of his tiny, brief pees, how once the stream made it all the way to her chin. And even though you think it is a little perverse how your sister is now unable to talk about anything but her son you want nothing more than to go to Ottawa and meet your first nephew.

You are in Ferdinand's bed when he says "deal-breaker." You are in bed discussing whether or not it is weird to have sex with his cat in the room and both of you think not in theory but maybe yes a little bit offputting and then he pops the door open because his cat—the mother he kept after giving away the remaining kittens—is scritching that she wants to get in. You are thinking how can you possibly love it so much, the way Ariel scritches your walls and door and furniture? You are wondering about the part of you that oozes rhapsodic and starts to mumble pettish pleasantries even when you are half-asleep and she claws the mirror until you get up to feed her and find her bowl still half-full. Your mind is purring softly through this Ariel montage when he says he has to tell you something and he hopes it isn't a deal-breaker. You're thinking marriage thinking AIDS thinking secret travelling salesman with alternate family thinking moving to Alaska or Australia and then you are trying to control your worst-case-scenario syndrome.

"Deal-breaker?" you laugh, summoning nonchalance. "I'm sure it's nothing."

"Well," he says, "maybe it's early for this but I've noticed the way you talk about your nephew and I just thought I should let you know that I don't want children."

A vast estrangement.

The world an explosion and you newly deaf. Everywhere soundless carnage.

"Oh, no, of course, whatever. No big deal."

If it's no big deal why are you resisting eye contact and letting him kiss you but feeling like his lips belong to a stranger or your long-lost biological brother. He asks are you sure and you say yes of course you're sure but just out of curiosity are you, Ferdinand, like a hundred percent about this? He says yes a hundred percent and you say just curious but why exactly and he tells you ecological reasons. He doesn't think he can justify bringing a child into this overpopulated world of depleting resources when there are so many children suffering and nothing could be more confusing because this is actually the kindest most logical answer you could imagine. You ask would he consider fostering or adopting and he says maybe and you once again find this strangely painful because you admire him so much but you know there is something inside you that can't be reasoned with and needs to see a version of yourself—your genome and your unpredictable hair and your tiny ears and all of your failures and problems—reflected imperfectly in the face of a tiny child. You tell him that's absolutely cool and actually you really respect his choice and then you force yourself to have sex with him again and this time it horrifies you that his cat is watching. You play normal for the rest of the night but on the walk home all you can think is *really?* Are you really going to break things off with this handsome perfect butcher because he doesn't want your snotty-nosed, genetically mediocre children?

When you get home and open your apartment door and the cat isn't there to greet you all you can do is slap the wall and count your breaths to suppress the panic. *One.* A bit older now, Ariel has been trying to get out the back door every time you open it. *Two.* You've been seriously considering it but haven't had the courage to let her into the yard yet. *Three.* So you are double-checking all the windows and thinking of who has a key to your place and obviously your mother wouldn't just come over and let the cat out to eff with you when you finally see her on the floor between the radiator and the couch. Your first reaction is enormous relief, swirling from your brain stem and sweetly kneading your clenched gut.

Then no. You are a single thought and that thought is a colossal no.

You are kneeling on the floor and touching her and petting her and checking gently for the pulse that you already know is not there. You have never felt a sadness so total. You are kneeling in some version of child's pose with both hands on your beloved, unbreathing cat, your body heaving and your lungs skittering and the snot seeming to crawl across your face and you have no idea who you are thinking to but all you can think is *let me make a bargain. Let me give this cat all of my breath and all of my blood. Let me divide my remaining years in two.* You would give everything now, you would sacrifice your very lifespan, to have this creature spasm and stand up and mewl and return everything to normal.

Instead the world is lost. The world is listing.

All your intuitions and miniscule decisions have tricked you and nothing remains but the booming thud of despair.

Once you and Ferdinand had talked about offshore. The two of you were lying on his perversely cozy flannel sheets and you'd mentioned you had a high-school friend who'd become an underwater welder at the Streamline project off Sable Island. "You know," Ferdinand said, "all that oil and gas goes right past us." You nodded although you'd had no idea and he went on about the pipeline, how it simply drifted right down into the States, probably passing over some traditional sacred Mi'kmaq land. Ferdinand said about this symptom, this faith in offshore oil and gas. He was talking and talking about this East Coast promise that had never been realized, saying how Nova Scotians would be paying into Streamline's pocket for years after the wells dried up, and you thought it was good that he was an idealist and that he cared about the causes and of course he was right. But you found yourself unmoved by the politics, found yourself just pondering the image of an offshore oil rig: iron legs stretching down to the continental shelf, schools of cod and mackerel nibbling the algae and kelp that grew on their great black knees. You were picturing a little flame down there in the wavering near-black, the blue-white nimbus bending metal in the murky subaqueous dark. You were dreaming the fallen ships of Sable Island, currents holding them against underwater mountainsides, algae and krill spawning from the remnants of human bodies long dead. And at the same time you were thinking upwards, above the surface. You were picturing horses, the famous wild horses of Sable Island. Ferdinand was talking pipelines and you were picturing horses galloping through the salt-gnawed grey.

You are running, now, up McDonald Bridge in the direction of Dartmouth. Running in your jeans and flats and are you running towards Ariel or away from her? The darkness is fading into day and you haven't slept and the clouds are moving fast, fast and silver over the harbour. There is a quivering quarter moon and you are running, panting, sprinting for the peak of the hill. Running has never felt so effortless and you feel there is something wrong, something ghostly. You are looking past the suicide rail into the sky and you do not know what you will do when you reach the top.

When you called Miranda instead of Ferdinand from the emergency vet's office you knew the deal was broken. She asked why he wasn't there and you blurted that he doesn't want babies and she said what and are you okay and you panicked and hung up and didn't answer any of her texts.

The vet said there was nothing you could have done. It was cardiomyopathy and it happens spontaneously and he was sorry but kittens sometimes just die. The vet suggested you could get another kitten and you vowed no, never. He mentioned "disposal" and you said no to that too. Said no to everything and forgot the cat carrier as you took the stiffening creature in your arms and walked away. Walked past the fake-smiling receptionist in her pink scrubs and carried Ariel back to your apartment where you dug a hole between the compost and the crumbling brown tulips. You set a cinder block over the grave and set off running, running in street clothes down the long hill towards the harbour and then back up through this great metal stitch in the midnight sky.

One of your flats wriggles off but you do not stop for it, keep running one-shoed. Approaching the apex of the bridge you are thinking of Ariel lying in the cool soil. You are thinking of Ariel and your calves are tiring as you reach the top of the hill and you look out over the moon-churning harbour and you keep running, running, galloping effortless. Ariel floats purringly in the air alongside but it is you galloping four-legged over the bridge that is no longer a bridge the wind in your hair and your hair becoming mane and beneath you oil runs through pipelines, runs deep underwater and welders wield thunderbolts in the liquid dark but how good it feels to run the full length of this marram-tufted sandbar, to run fast and weightless, almost flying, hooves kissing nimble over sandy wet earth.

HORSE PEOPLE

FRIDAY

The Manager of Jumping calls and asks me to wiggle his mouse around, which at first I think is sexual. But then he says seriously. There's an emergency at home and he wants me to go into his office every fifteen-twenty to jiggle the mouse around, maybe tap a few keys. "There are monitors," he says. "Denise gets alerts. I know this is weird but if you want my recommendation for that position in Dressage." I'm not sure I want his recommendation but I write down his door code (0000) and computer password (Hor$edude) and walk into the office with the pictures of his hairdresser wife and pageant-prim daughters grinning together, their mouths full of cantaloupe. I sit cruising his mouse around its pad and then I'm logging in. I think about searching the hard drive or the browser history but decide I don't want to find anything dark and still have to smile as I stare into his Belmont-browned teeth.

I'm drifting the cursor around a pixelated beachscape—a confetti of desktop icons amid tiki huts and plastic cups—when Denise raps on the glass. It is presumably less than ideal to have the CEO knocking on the big open window that looks onto a carpeted hallway, the window with blinds that I did not think to close. It's not great to have the CEO observe me illegally shifting office habitats to undertake phony computer activity and then Denise walks right in.

"He asked you to come in and move his mouse around?"

I nod into Denise's tectonic jaw.

"Pinkiedicked shithole." I must look stunned because she says, "Off the record but true—he's a scandalous manwhore." The Manager of Jumping, she explains, has been "liaising" with the breeder from Barbados who was in for a presentation yesterday, the one with the upturned nose. Denise tells me "just between us girls" that the snout-nosed breeder is also a married woman. Then she tells me to get back to my cubicle, pulling out her phone to call the Manager of Jumping. I head to my desk and sit checking horse passports and listening to the squirrel rucking around the ceiling panels.

The Manager of Jumping calls toilet paper "shit tickets." The Manager of Jumping's favourite casual Friday T-shirt says "I Support the Performing Arts" next to a swervy cartoon butt in a sequined green G-string. The Manager of Jumping is actually named Chad Tucker but I prefer to think of him as the Manager of Jumping because when I told Pierce his job title there was some confusion and then various running jokes about the Superintendent of Leaping, Le Directeur de Sauté. The Manager of Jumping pronounces minestrone "mine stroan." The Manager of Jumping uses "gay" as a pejorative. Once Denise asked if he was a homophobe and he went pale before blurting "No I'm not you're the friggin' homo." The Manager of Jumping has almost no lips and one of those beardless male faces with marble-cake swirls of blush, as if he were constantly exercising. The Manager of Jumping is generally disliked in the office but the Manager of Jumping has been here twenty-seven years. The Manager of Jumping had not yet learned my name when he walked into my cubicle and without pretence asked about my left ear. "How'd you get that prune ear?" Which what if I'd been born like this? What if it was a birth defect? What if I'd emerged from the womb with an extra pinkie or a huge purple birthmark on my face? I suspect that in each case the Manager of Jumping would have walked directly over and asked me to account for my abnormalities.

At lunch Denise is no longer serious Denise. She is now pregnancy fairy godmother Denise, giggling over to put a hand on my medicine ball belly as I'm trying to gorge rigatoni. I guess I'm showing the embarrassment because she gives the chin-jut that means female solidarity then says, "It's okay hon you're eating for two." She pats my stomach-flesh and smiles as if the two of us are syncopated, our cycles linked by the secret language of the moon. And then it's the urgent "you look *so good*" that makes me suspect the opposite. So I'm sitting there eating a rigatoni that's gone tasteless and wondering why everyone particularly older women feel suddenly permitted to prod and rub and vocalize about my body just because I'm growing a miniature human. Like the body suddenly becomes a public archive with everyone asking "how are you feeling?" and grimacing when I ask them back. People asking how am I feeling and what they really want to know is how are the hemorrhoids, how much have your nipples darkened, how does it feel to wake up in the middle of the night to find a weep of colostrum drying on your upper arm.

Denise asks how far along now and I tell her thirty-two weeks without mentioning that she asked this question yesterday and the answer was the same. She coos and rubs her model-sharp jaw and tells me about Horace, how he spent the whole third trimester standing on her bladder. "He was really just perched on my pee-pump," she says, adding that by the time she had her pants back on she always needed to pee again and even though he felt like a cheese grater coming through her perineum she'd do it again in a heart murmur—"at the wink of a ventricle." We laugh and then she tells me to get back to work. "Don't you have some horse passports to vet?" She juts her formidable chin in the way that means she is joking and not joking, joking but don't push your luck.

People end up working at the Canadian Equine Federation because they're horse people. They go for a career at the Federation because they grow up with their knees turned sideways in the backs of Toyota Tundras and Ford Rangers. They come here because they love the warm reek of fresh manure, because they know that sheep dung is the best fertilizer and round bales are better than square. They come here because they loved using the curry brush on an irascible sorrel gelding named Chewbacca while the inbred kittens scurried around their aunt's barn leaking from their distempered sockets. They come here because they like to watch barrel racing and the six horse hitch and The Mane Event. They end up here because maybe being an Olympian didn't work out and then being a vet didn't work out and being an admin assistant for the Federation with maybe the possibility of one day travelling to the Olympics looked a lot better than answering phones for a wholesale vacuum company or labelling porn videos according to sex act. They come here because they are horse people, soil people, country people, people with mud on their boots and a saddle that never leaves their back seat and horsehair all over the upholstery. They end up becoming Chads and Denises. They end up writing memos about budget synchronicity and brand revitalization and the toxic culture of tardiness. They end up saying they have a nut allergy and although this has never been confirmed with an actual allergic reaction it means nobody in the office can brush lip or eyelash to walnut or pistachio. These sometime horse people end up spending forty plus per week in a building with fully regulated temperatures, a building where you cannot open the windows because they are barred from the outside, a building where the AC is cranked so high people sit around their cubicles wearing sweaters on a thirty-three-degree July afternoon. These animal lovers spend one hour per week debating the relative merits of allowing employees' pet dogs into the office, finally deciding no on the grounds of cleanliness and preferential treatment, on the grounds that Meredith's dog is twice the size of Antoine's so mess-wise it really wouldn't be equitable. These people who grew up thriving on hay and muck and trying not to crush the new chicklets while they walked through their dirt-patch spend their lives staring at emails and PowerPoints and using words like "synergy" and "innovation" without ever wondering what they mean.

The Manager of Jumping appears after lunch, unshaven and smelling of hotel champagne. He blusters over to my cubicle and does not thank me for the mouse wiggling but instead opens his practically lipless mouth and says WTF. He does not say "what the fuck" although that would require fewer syllables. "WTF Trace," he says, his red face turning redder. His teeth stained with lipstick or strawberries. "What's that sound?" He points up towards a corner of the ceiling and I'm wordless until I realize I'd been blocking out the scratches and patters of our new ceiling rodent. I tell him it's the squirrel. It's been there all day. I explain that the squirrel must've burrowed inside somehow after Denise had that tumour-pocked tree removed from the outskirts of the parking lot. The Manager of Jumping does not like this explanation. The Manager of Jumping hisses "vermin" and spends the rest of the afternoon standing on various chairs around the office, using a snow shovel to pry the ceiling panels. No rodents fall from the vent-shaft and the sound does not stop and eventually it's cake time, either because it's somebody's birthday or because tasteless white sugar cake on Fridays seems to be part of the office's Mandate of Bland.

How I got the prune ear was a grandmotherly Palomino named Luna. Luna got an infection and lost her eye so my aunt Shelly got her for a couple of haybales and none of the students wanted to ride her so I did. I was thirteen and eager to have my own horse so I led her and worked her and trotted her around the ring. She was easy and docile and although she could barely muster a canter I was thrilled to take care of her.

One day I startled her putting her summer blanket on and she nipped me. When you're with a horse you have to make sure it sees you, which means you move gently to the side, where the eyes are. This time I forgot about the bad eye and so I was standing to her left without thinking maybe she didn't see me. I came around to the right and I must have moved too fast because she flinched and kicked the back wall and then bit me in the ear. Not hard—something between a fear bite and a curiosity bite—but her teeth were hard and my ear went loud and numb and I could feel the blood leaking out, could hear it drizzling onto my shoulder. Strangely I did not run or scream. I did not dart away or call for my aunt because after she bit me I turned to look at Luna and I saw the pupil gaping in her amber eye, saw the fear pulsing in that great brown ocean. I stayed there dripping blood onto the shoulder of my denim jacket and humming to Luna, clucking and shushing and feeding her hairy carrot ends, telling her it was okay, that she was okay. I came up to Shelly blood-soaked with a hand cupped over my ear and we jumped in the Dodge and headed for the hospital. As I sat there watching silos and rotten barns whip by the shock faded and the pain came on loud and dazzling and Shelly told me it was alright, that you're not a real horse person until you've got a nice mean scar.

Pierce is making stroganoff and drinking bourbon and when I come in to spoon some sauce from the pot he promises not to make the stroking off joke. I tell him that's cheating and he holds the bourbon in front of my nose the way I like. "Peaty, eh?"

I ask whether anyone actually knows what peat smells or tastes like or do they get their idea of peat-smell from whiskey. "You know peat is actually what preserved the bog people?"

Pierce says that's what he loves about me and turns away to plate the strog. I monopolize dinner conversation, complaining about the em of jay for a while then moving on to the squirrel. Pierce says maybe we can talk about what you like about your job which is really infuriating because isn't it his duty to listen to me complain, to be on my side.

No, he says, that's not his duty. His duty is to keep me grounded and support me. "Seriously, what do you like about your job?"

"Mat leave. Benefits."

"If you hate it so much you can quit."

"Quit at seven months pregnant?"

He tells me sure, tells me he will support me with his freelance editing and his mandolin lessons and we laugh but then he says he's serious.

"It's just sometimes I miss working with actual horses."

He says I should do what I love, that we can get a line of credit. I tell him he's sweet and he's an idiot and there's no way I'm quitting my government job.

After dinner Pierce pours me my three-ounce-glass of merlot. I'm in the third trimester now so I get a three-ounce pour on Wednesday and Friday and sometimes Sunday. I like to drink it after dinner, to relax with it fully sated.

Pierce stands up to do the dishes and I tell him my theory about the horse people, how my co-workers start out horse people and end up email addicted budget police.

"Houyhnhnms!" he shouts.

I stare into the cherry-dark loveliness of my wine and wait for him to continue.

"Houyhnhnms," he says again, looking at me like he expects me to know what it means. When I tell him I don't he goes bright and cackle-shouts, "*Gulliver's Travels*?" I shake my head and he runs off towards his office, suds luffing off his fingertips. He returns saying he can't find the book but I have to read it.

We watch *Planet Earth* in bed until Pierce falls asleep and I lie there envying his big unimpeded lungs and trying to remember the great formless emptiness of a good sleep. Eventually I rise to pee and then I clean the glasses off our nightstands, take them into the kitchen and stand there looking into the bourbon bottle.

I dream the baby staring at me. It is somehow in the womb and looking at me with wideset alien eyes. Its skin is translucent and its head is enormous and despite the ultrasound results it is neither boy nor girl, neither male nor female. It is far too alien for that. It is glowing and womb-pink and see-through and it sits in the uterus cross-legged, the fleshy cave rising up over its head like a throne. There are chicken-scratch scrawlings on the womb wall which in the dream I find a bit unsettling. Like maybe the child is far too smart, like maybe this extraterrestrial baby is chagrined by something, chagrined and scheming. But mostly what I sense is intelligence.

Intelligence and curiosity coming through, almost incomprehensible, from the far side of a fleshy barrier that is not the difference between life and death but between life and life.

SATURDAY

I wake up with a soft headache and a tender dehydration and the feeling is familiar, the vague shame and depletion of a hangover. It is recognizable and not so bad but then it is acute and awful, more awful than a hangover has ever been. Especially as I rise to pee and feel myself waddling, my hands instinctively reaching for the bulge of my gestating child. The feeling becomes increasingly horrific as I remember Pierce going to bed early, recall sneaking into the kitchen for a second three-ounce Merlot and then a golden twinkle of bourbon, lovely and wretched. And this mnemonic murk sharpens into a poison of guilt as the unborn child in me starts to move and kick then gets what I used to think were hiccups but now think are prison-break-mother-hating rage-punches. I sit on the toilet long after I've finished, sit there just feeling this vile riptide of guilt and thinking of my irreparably damaged child, thinking of my baby blooming a spina bifida cauliflower between her shoulder blades. I'm seeing a parade of busted neural tubes, a cackling carousel of helpless mutant babies, feeling weak and hurt and horrid, wanting so badly to share my pain with Pierce but not knowing how.

Sometimes this goop would pour out of Luna's eye socket, milk-white pus that looked like android blood from *Aliens*. The socket was wide open and you could see deep into it— the strange wet opening like the roof of a mouth, the red-blue scraggle of veins, the useless twitch of optical nerves. At first I worried it was prone to infection but when I asked Shelly she said the best thing for it was the open air. She said you could cover it or stick a fake eyeball in there but there was nothing you could really do to fix it—it would always be a septic wound. She figured it was best not to let anything fester. The socket was a great home for bacteria. "If it's moving in," she grinned, "it better be paying rent."

Sometimes, especially if it was windy or the temperature changed abruptly, this milk-goop would leak from the socket and I would wipe it up for her. Not wanting to reach right into the cavity, I'd wait until the goo dripped out and then I'd wipe it from the socket's lip. When I did this I'd stare straight into that crimson concavity. I would gaze into that open unhealable wound and marvel at it. How strange, I thought then, to look into the place where an eye should be and see only flesh. And somehow I could never accept that there was not something there, something beholding me, recognizing me—something looking back.

Maybe I didn't fully realize that getting pregnant meant getting sober, like totally, terribly, sober. More likely I didn't realize that fortyish weeks is a seriously long time to be sober. Perhaps I didn't realize that I'd been slowly listing towards boozebaggery for a decade give or take. Like partying every weekend at twenty-one turns into partying four nights a week at twenty-five turns into "wining down" every night and it's not drinking alone because Pierce is there. And then a sudden prohibition like zero tolerance for the first trimester and it's not like I craved a drink but I missed it. It had become a treat, a ritual, and a person needs treats, needs rituals. But maybe I didn't realize that the complete cut-off would be shocking and that I would crave the ceremony of it and yes I might even miss the odd moment of abandon, of having a bath or lying on the couch and saying fuck it. Part of me was afraid of becoming like my not-quite-functioning alcoholic friends back home—drinking hangover Caesars and 3 p.m. casuals and white wine from a sippy cup because what kind of cop's going to pull you over and check your sippy cup when you've got a toddler in the car seat. Maybe I don't want to end up like that but I also don't want to be sober, I don't want to be an adult, I don't want to live in a world where making one dumb mistake means ruining someone else's life and having to live with that. But it's finished now. It's finished and it's too late to lie awake at night thinking *what have I done?* Too late but that doesn't stop me.

Pierce and I walk down to Mud Lake and there's a pair of cardinals there in the stark March branches and I'm wondering if he's noticed the missing three fingers of bourbon yet and whether I should tell him before he does. Pierce puts out his finger and a downy woodpecker flutters right down and sits on it but all he can say is "cardinal." The woodpecker flaps away and Pierce says something about a skybound rose but I'm not looking at the bright red cardinal. I'm looking at the female, the colour of bark with a twinge of red on her beak and tail. I'm looking at this grey-brown female bird and thinking how she is the object of all the male's beauty, that she is the end goal of his dazzle. And what does he see in her, this livid-red male who must be totally enthralled with her understated charm.

"Isthmus," Pierce says into the March chill.

I look at him like "what?" and he says, "Narrow body of land surrounded by water, joining two larger pieces of land." He's practising for one of his freelance jobs, the one where he makes lists of words for a dictionary website. Lists like "five wacky weather words" and "three words to tank your cover letter."

"We just called it the armpit of the peninsula."

He looks at me like he's surprised that I know the word already so I tell him if there's anything you learn growing up in the Wentworth Valley it's the word "isthmus." When your grandfather drives groomers at the Wentworth ski hill, you know the word "isthmus." When people say "the city" and it's unclear if they mean Moncton or Halifax, you know the word "isthmus." I rub my belly and tell him that I basically am an isthmus.

Pierce says that's what he loves about me and as usual he means it. But today the comment just stirs the wretched brew of guilt. We walk home along the river trail, look out over the sprawling woebegone of late March ice. A rotten snows-cape chanting *bourbon*, whispering *failure*, and I am longing to confess but remaining quiet and sullen and lonely even as Pierce walks beside me, breaking into a jovial impromptu song about the luckiest cardinal in the world.

I go upstairs for a nap and find a copy of *Gulliver's Travels* on my pillow. I read the dustjacket and stare into the crudely drawn maps and then skim from Lilliputians to Houyhnhnms. The story starts off strange and fascinating but soon turns into Gulliver explaining the inanities of Queen Anne's England to an aristocratic rational horse. Though the horse does not even understand the concept of clothes, I picture him wearing tails and a monocle. I picture him grinning and avuncular, benev-olent as a Georgian plantation master. And of course it turns out that the Houyhnhnms keep slaves and practise eugenics AKA human breeding so I drift back to sleep thinking *horse people, horse people*.

Before I got my job at the Federation I taught riding lessons at a stable in Kenora, which meant I still felt like a horse person. Not the same horse person who lifted bales and casu-ally stomped garter snakes at her aunt's farm. Not the same horse person who snuggled inbred barn kittens in the hay loft, holding their mutated paws and letting them lick her with their splinter-gruff tongues. Not the horse person who galloped across an open pasture looking out at the valley and breathing a wind thick with Fundy's salt caress. This was a horse person who taught ten-to-thirteen-year-olds from the Glebe how to get a boot into a stirrup, how to swing their right leg overtop of a rheumatic Arabian named Perseus and keep their hands loose on the reins. This was the horse person who held a lead and chanted "heels down" and "confirmation" and "it's a conversation don't forget to listen." Back then my back seat still held a Troxel and an old stained saddle pad and the upholstery was clotted with different shades of horsehair and on the way home my car was rich with the smell of hay and manure. I'd often roll down the window to let the air in and I'd just sit there smiling with the sun on my face, not knowing or caring why.

I'm in bed tumbling through internet holes when I get a text from Denise: the word "Oregon!" above a picture of the Manager of Jumping grinning brattishly, a hairy tuft of kale clenched in his right incisor. Repulsed as I am, I keep staring because I'm trying to parse the word "Oregon." So I keep looking and puzzling and then I notice that the picture's a photoshop job—the Manager of Jumping's face has been grafted onto a pregnant woman's body. A pregnant woman's body that I eventually realize is my pregnant woman's body. I'm combing this image trying to figure out what exactly is so unnerving about the Manager of Jumping's ruddy lipless face fused onto my pregnant body and then I see it: the Manager of Jumping has "pregnancy glow," the storied brightness I've never managed to attain. The deep corrosive horror in me is that the Manager of Jumping looks somehow right, somehow perfect, somehow flourishing as a pregnant lady.

I'm lying there staring at this picture in a wretched frantic trance when I get a follow-up text that says "sorry Oregon supposed to be prego damn autocorrect" and as I'm parsing this semantic masterpiece I get another text asking if I could please send out a reminder email about Monday's budget meeting. "NBD but if you want that job in Dressage your going to have to start talking some initiative."

I dream the baby with a tail. I dream the baby floating in utero with hooves and a tail and not in a good way. Not at all in a good way and my horse-human fetus has enormous brown eyes with no sclera and it's a girl now, definitively a horsegirl. My horsedaughter looks at me and leans close, leans very close in order to whisper through the amniotic fluid and what she says is *it's us. It's us, Mum, we are the horse people.* In the dream this makes total sense. In the dream this is a revelation and everything becomes love, an insanity of love and I am trying to pick up my beloved child to bring her close and tell her yes of course, trying and trying but I can't get close enough. In the dream I feel a craze of love for this out-of-reach child but when I wake up I'm nagged for hours by a strange and nameless murk, a distant cloying shame.

SUNDAY

Place the blueberry into your vagina. The instructor is saying to put the blueberry into your vagina and hold it there. Squeeze the blueberry gingerly. Cradle it in the labia. Do not squish it, do not let it fall. Cradle it in the vagina, really nestle it.

The instructor is saying this to twelve women lying spread eagle, propped up by bolsters and splaying their legs out and I've never really thought about the term "spread eagle" before but now I see it: twelve women with their lower limbs perched in the air looking like a fleet of soaring birds and I am sweating and hungry, suddenly ravenous for blueberries.

During Shavasana the instructor says think purple thoughts, send soothing energy to your baby so of course I go straight to the bourbon. A gaggle of gestating humans tilted up on bolsters and we are supposed to be cultivating peace and stillness for our babies but I'm shamefully recalling the sear of bourbon in my throat. Then I'm remembering the baby book, how it said a little alcohol is okay. The book written by a Fulbright Scholar and cancer researcher who is also a mother and she said about correlation. All the studies are based around correlation not causality and there are also studies that suggest that mothers who have one alcoholic drink per day have smarter babies so there's really just no way of knowing. The doctors say zero is best because FAS is real and awful and saying zero is the best way to protect people with low impulse control. But there is nothing conclusive and probably a little bit of alcohol is fine, especially in the third trimester. Even a little bit of hard liquor is probably not devastating and surely people have done much much worse and still produced healthy babies so why am I thinking strabismus? Why am I lying here in Shavasana picturing horns and extra digits and a heart beating outside a body? Why am I just now remembering "horseshoe kidney," a FAS-related condition where the child's kidneys fuse together? Why am I recalling or possibly inventing the fact that when someone has horseshoe kidney the space where the two organs join is called the "isthmus"?

The instructor comes around spraying tea tree mist and I feel her hovering near me, placing a hand on my stomach. She chirps "aren't you cute as a button?" which ruins the already-compromised yoga trance. Seeing her this close I notice that her face has the same ruddy redness in the cheeks as the Manager of Jumping. She even has the same frowning unibrow, the same nearly lipless mouth.

Addressing everyone again, the instructor beams about the light in me and the light in you and although I usually shudder at this particular ritual of cultural tourism this time I succumb. I hear myself whispering, not as a gratitude to the beaming kerchiefed instructor but as a plea to my gestating liquor-sodden child: *namaste.*

There is a strange March warmth building so Pierce and I walk out into the backyard and just stand there in the open grey. Pierce says "petrichor" and when I ask what he means he wheels a hand around his nose. "The smell. It comes from the soil. Most people think it only happens after the rain but actually that chemical is released before precipitation as well." So we stand there together smelling the petrichor and I think how that pre-rain smell is more beautiful now that I know its name.

Pierce asks me to tell him again about the private jet so I say how people know about the horse semen. It's basically common knowledge that a dose of sperm from a retired champion thoroughbred is worth a hundred thousand plus. What people don't know about is the private jet. One reason horses need passports is for competitions like the Olympics. Another is the horse sex plane, the private jet full of stallions that travels pretty much non-stop so that these horses can exit the plane and inseminate a mare in Perth one day, Singapore the next. And why not just mail the semen? Why not just use AI? Because organizations like the Jockey Club—the governing body of American horse racing—make "live cover" mandatory for all registered foals. "Live cover" being a euphemism for physical sex. All of this ensuring stallion and mare breed through intercourse rather than with human extraction of horse semen through artificial horse vagina. Stallion sex plane or human-horse hand jobs and subsequent semen injection. Those are the two options and neither seems exactly sane.

Pierce is doing his scrunch-think face, which is not his most attractive face but nonetheless it feels good to make someone's brain flex. "So it's like animals having orgasms and humans making money off those orgasms and the stallions never get to see their children or even know they have any offspring. And the mothers carry those babies for eleven or twelve months and then look after them for a few and pass them off to some fascistic trainer and most people just walk around thinking this is completely fine."

I tell him yes and we stand there in the windy desolation, contemplating horse semen and stallion sex planes. I'm once again thinking *tell him tell him tell him* and eventually thinking *why am I not telling him?* We head inside and lie on the bed watching raindrops ticker off the skylight.

On the message board there's a post titled "Did I Cook My Baby?" There's a woman who took to the internet frantic because she stood in front of a hot element for five minutes and when she walked away her stomach was hot to the touch. Of course she put ice on it right away but could someone please reassure her that she did not cook her baby. Someone has responded that maybe six minutes would have cooked baby but with five she should be fine. Which is maybe a bit mean but also funny and what the whole thing gets me thinking about is paranoia. The baby book says it's common to worry about birth defects but for the most part the worry is irrational. Pierce would probably tell me I'm being paranoid. Pierce would say it will be fine, in all likelihood our child will be completely undamaged—plucky and hale. Pierce would say forget about it, our baby will be lovely, our baby will be beautiful and even if there's something wrong we are going to shower it in delirious narcotic love and there's nothing else we can or will do but meet it and care for it and love it to excess. Pierce would say all this and it would make me feel better so why am I not telling Pierce?

The same spring Luna bit me we learned that she was pregnant, had most likely been sold to my aunt pregnant. We were surprised that at twenty-five Luna was still capable of settling. Shelly said I could help her and the vet deliver the baby which mostly meant filling bucket after bucket of water and occasionally running to get ointment and latex gloves from the vet's Silverado. This was not the first time I'd seen it but it was nonetheless astounding when the vet slid her right arm up to the shoulder in Luna's anus. First the vet's eyes were taut and curious as if she were surveying a sprawling vista. I asked what she was doing and she said "just looking around" and I pictured eyeballs on the end of her latexed fingertips, gazing around the rectal depths. She said okay let's give her some privacy so we cleaned out the empty stalls while we listened for Luna to lie down and start pushing.

Her labour took a massive ten minutes and then the foal came out feet first, covered in a milk-white sac that the vet removed. The foal was gangly and wet and its coat was rich chestnut and it wasn't moving. Luna shuffled around in the hay until she was able to nuzzle her foal but it stayed still, terribly still. The vet wasn't doing anything and my aunt hooked her thumbs in her beltloops and I was saying why is it not moving, why is it not moving. The women did not answer and they did not need to and the three of us stood there in the stall watching Luna lick her child's muzzle—licking and nudging that motionless foal, nuzzling slower and slower until finally she rolled away, sounding one deep groan then fluttering her eyes and finally closing them, submitting to sleep.

In the dream I'm in a studio full of jacked, muscular women and I'm a horrible soft blob and Denise is in front of me and she has no legs. Denise is doing a perfect bridge and she has no legs, just four corked and double-jointed arms. She also has two heads, both of them turning to glare into me and then the back head which is also sprouting out of some sort of a shoulder cleft butt crack becomes Chad's face. Four-armed bridging Denise/Chad scuttles closer to me and then Denise's face grins wide-eyed and says "mommy brain," says "prego," says "budget," after which Chad's head squeals "WTF" and "aren't you cute as a button?" Then both of them start jabbering "Dressage Dressage Dressage" at which point they seem to want me to jump onto the fused isthmus of their back so I do. I leap on and dig into the stirrups and they keep chanting "Dressage" and bucking like a rodeo bull and I'm thinking this can't be good for the baby but what else can I do but clutch the mane and cling on.

MONDAY

The Manager of Jumping dances up to my desk playing a flute of chocolate ex-lax. "Squirrel," he says gleefully but it takes me a minute to draw the connection. It takes until I watch the Manager of Jumping head to each corner of the room raising four of the spongy office ceiling panels and sliding several cubes of ex-lax into each one for me to realize that what he means is that he's attempting to poison the squirrel. He twinkles about the office, humming dreamily as he stands on wheeled chairs to raise the ceiling squares, his dress shirt rising to show a little gust of undershirt, the fungal-pink frown of his love handles. Scanning my computer I see that it's 9:22 a.m. I have never seen the Manager of Jumping in the office this early or this happy.

The first thing Denise says when she arrives at 10:15 is that I look like a vampire. She gnaws a piece of stale Friday cake and says I look vampirish. "Not a sexy vampire either— sorry hon but you're no Buffy. Are you sleeping?" I tell her no

I'm not sleeping too well and she says "welcome to the third trimester" and I realize that all of this was set-up to a scripted story about her pregnancy—how she didn't sleep for four months and if I think I'll catch up *after* baby comes I'm in for a real rutabaga.

She sits down at the corner of my desk and puts a hand on my belly, looks genuinely concerned as she tells me I've dropped. "You were carrying so high and now"—she cups her breasts hard, lets them collapse—"it's all sinking. Oh, the erosion that is my life."

I can't tell if she's joking so I try a sympathetic half-laugh and turn back to the horse passports. But Denise stays perched on my desk, doing email on her phone which why doesn't she just go to her computer? "Mommy brain," Denise says. She takes her last bite of cake and then says while sucking on a finger that the mommy brain explains why I hit "reply" instead of "reply all" on that innocuous email. I do not tell her not to say "mommy brain" loud enough that the men can hear it. I conjure a sisterly smile and tell her yeah she's probably right. Then she stands, dusts a colony of crumbs towards my cubicle, and heads for her office.

At eleven fifteen a man walks into the office holding a metal wand and saying his name is Ernesto from Barbados and where is Chawed? A full-mouthed man with flared jeans and designer sunglasses. He speaks in a warped British accent, saying he came all the way from Barbados to get violent with Chawed. I'm softly bouncing on my yoga ball and clenching my thighs as I watch this man swing his metal rod around and it takes me a while to realize it's a putter. It takes until he holds it with two hands over my computer and says he will begin to break things, he will drive this putter into someone's eye socket if I do not tell him where Chawed that little puto is hiding. Things do not clarify until I receive an email alert from Chad Tucker and the subject line reads "REMAIN CLAM AUTHORITIES ALTERED."

For some reason I acquiesce. For some reason I remain calm as I scan the office and see that I am the only one still at my desk. Perhaps I assume nobody would assault a pregnant lady but in any case I remain calm as I turn to the conference room and see a dozen eyes peering back through the slits in the blinds. Eyes that belong to Denise and the Manager of Jumping among others. I tell this caustic golfer that Chad is out of the office and the authorities have been called and it's up to him if he would prefer to leave of his own accord or wait for the police.

He broils closer with a gust of hate. Then he pulls the putter back fast and I cover my face as the club cuts down and digs into my computer monitor, sends a scuttle of broken glass across my desk. I stand up feeling a shard dig into my heel-flesh as Ernesto swings again, this time denting the wall of my cubicle. Fibreboard mists around me and the world seems to wobble and tilt and something hefty flubs out of the ceiling. At first I think the building is collapsing but then I see the white-streaked tail and the horrid jagged teeth of a squirrel.

Ernesto drops to his knees and leans over the stiff little rodent, cursing quietly. This is when I see that the squirrel is covered in a slick travesty of feces and that it is female, nipples oozing chalk-white loam.

Something about this dead and dripping squirrel placates Ernesto. He kneels in front of it almost religiously, his curses becoming gentler, almost tender as he stares into its white-streaked tail, its milk-caked nipples, the total blackness of its dead, dead eyes. Eventually he scoops the squirrel up like an offering, walks away without a glance or a word.

The Manager of Jumping orders pizza and we eat it in complete silence. Nobody thanks me for confronting Ernesto or filling out the police report but it doesn't matter because I am not here. I am driving with Shelly on a secondary highway outside Pictou, watching a chestnut Arabian named Chamomile spill out from the back doors of the trailer as we drive away from a cavernous pothole. I am sitting with Shelly listening to Shania and watching in the side mirror as the trailer gate shudders and snaps open and Chamomile drifts out dreamlike, scrabbling for purchase on the yellow line. She seems to be flying, soaring backward over the tarmac and Shelly is braking but still getting farther and farther away until the horse is a tiny helpless speck in the shifting light of dusk.

We went back that day. We did a youie and drove back down the desolate salt-wracked road and found Chamomile basically unharmed. We got her into the trailer and roped it shut and got her home fine except for a few scuffs and some shock but what has always fascinated me is that glimpse of her in the rear-view, all the stability she'd taken for granted suddenly wrenched away. I think of her standing there in the trailer one moment and then inexplicably lost to the open, soaring highway. And what is that but the way all of us live— the trailer seeming stable until it is not, until we are released to fly fast and off-balance with no purchase or handhold.

By one thirty there are baby squirrels dropping from the roof. Four baby squirrels fall in succession from the still-displaced ceiling panels and land on the carpet writhing and shuddering. At first I think they're twitching from the impact but then I remember the mother squirrel with the loam of milk on her swollen teats and I realize they are starving. The Manager of Jumping approaches gleefully announcing that the ex-lax worked. Then he raises a shoe and stomps, crushing the head of a twitching baby. Trust me: I am no squirrel lover. Back home squirrels are cute and russet and fearful as they scamper about the woods. Here they are tar-black and beast-ly, a stoned belligerence in their disease-reddened eyes. But imagine. Imagine there is a little writhing cluster of starving infant squirrels. Imagine they are hideous, like tiny red-eyed wingless bats. Then imagine your superior raises his Rockport and brings the heel down while Denise cackles behind him, her canines dark with lipstick smear. What compassionate person would not tell Chad that he is filth, that he is a cold sore on the mouth of the human species? What caring and sane individual would not stare fiercely at the Manager of Jumping as he stammers something about having her fired, would not calmly pronounce that she would gladly choose a squirrel's life over his? What decent person would do anything other than pick up the three shuddering and barely conscious squirrels and cradle them into her purse while walking away, not answering the Manager of Jumping as he shouts down the hall about "protocol" and "accountability"?

At home I hand Pierce the squirrels and he takes them with-out question, starts setting up a little den in his underwear drawer. I tell him I might have quit my job and he says re-ally and I say no, I don't know. He hugs me and says that's great either way and then rushes to the pet store and comes back with formula and a syringe and we spend the evening siphoning pseudo-milk into squirrel mouths and asking the internet about how to care for baby rodents. Gradually they stop twitching. They lie there stuporish for a while and then seem to recover to relative infant squirrel normality. We put them back in the underwear drawer, cracking it a little for oxygen. They peep for a while then go quiet and I lie there in the darkness feeling the baby turning and hiccupping, hoping the squirrels aren't dead.

It's late when Pierce wakes me up. There's lightning twitch-ing across the skylight and I'm thinking *really* then thinking *yes* and it's like it used to be four years ago when we started dating. Hands warm no hot and there is a tongue and more lightning and Pierce is whispering something about entering the isthmus and gently licking my damaged ear. It is never intentional or really arousing but sometimes while I'm having sex I think about the first time I galloped. Sometimes I have a visceral involuntary memory of looking down past the barn to the blueberry fields where that skulking abused German Shepherd snarled at passersby. I sense my own two legs disappearing into the four legs beneath them, feel myself and Genesis thudding along right there in the bed and all the trees and the fenceposts and the clouds are speeding by faster than life and love, faster than hope and loss and possibility. The air is bright and full and everything is brilliant so fast too fast and brilliant and beneath me the hooves thundering thundering hooves and I am flying racing zooming not just over the landscape but along the very brink of control, away from control and steering and the need to ever think about slowing down.

Everyone says sex is okay when you're pregnant. The experts insist that sex while pregnant is okay, even beneficial, and then it turns out it's not. It turns out there is more blood than I've ever seen before, blood like *The Shining*. Blood that is dark and true and the fierce fetid smell of it and what it smells like is bodies, flesh, wet dredged earth.

Pierce was working faster and faster but still tender, still gentle, which was when I felt something wrong. I felt a strange unpleasant heat and I told Pierce to get out and then yelled at him to turn on the lights and I knew already but still was not prepared for the absurdity of red that bloomed across the bed, a catastrophe of red beneath the stark electric light.

It is a strange thing lying here in the hospital bed with the toothpaste-green shower curtain, nurses and doctors drifting through to look up my gown into a mangled genital hinterland. It is a strange thing being sure I am giving birth and knowing it's going badly but also being in Shelley's barn with the rusted Toyota and the inbred cats and signed poster of Ian Millar. It is strange that even as I am looking at a body diagram on the wall and noticing that there is something called the "isthmus" of the fallopian tube I am also in the stall where Luna gave birth and she is there as well, even though she died four months after she birthed the stillborn foal. I'm labouring as horses do, lying on my side, and what I feel is not pain but an enormous need, an enormous gift blooming out of me. I'm pushing and pushing and wondering where the pain is, when is the pain going to come and somewhere I hear Pierce whispering *isthmus*, saying don't worry the squirrels are safe and nourished, telling me I'm the join between him and the baby so I'm going to be alright, I need to be alright. I mutter something about the bourbon and he says he knows, has always known. He says it's okay, maybe don't do it again but just this once he's sure it's fine. Then he's whispering *isthmus my beautiful isthmus you are going to be such a good mother* but his voice is small and cartoony, far away from the barn where Luna comes closer, wearing mom jeans and a floral blouse, a black suede jacket with a tan dangle of fringe. The jeans are up above her waist and her pubic roll is formidable and lovely and she is reaching out her hand, her hand which is somehow both hooved and fingered and the hoof-hand is holding a scalpel and taking my hand gently and I am pushing, pushing huge and painless and breathing hard and Luna is grinning and nuzzling me and saying *look, look.* So I sit up and stare down between my legs and watch as something red pours out of me. Something livid and red and it is liquid then it is a rose. An insanity of redness between my legs and the redness begins to flap, rises as the rose turns bird, flutters up, up, flails about to face me. Hovers there becoming visage and it's a face I recognize, a face I have always known and I am thinking yes, yes, it's you. Of course it is you. It has always been you and you are perfect and you are mine, perfectly mine.

PENINSULA SINKING

BELLYFLOP

What if it had been you, that day at the pool with Drew and Theo, and you'd bumped into Jen Hamilton and Tessa Brown? What if you'd never met Jen and Tessa before that day because they went to Cornwallis but you'd heard about Jen getting Eric Doan to finger her under the blanket at Drew's house last Halloween while everyone was watching *Scream 2*? What if Drew hugged her by the waterslide and then introduced you and you were showing off your backflips for a while before Tessa and Jen started giggling and pointing at your crotch. What if the words "baby carrot" were used? What if Jen's voice had that weird pool echo and you suspected that everyone—the lithe blond lifeguard and the little girls wearing water wings and the Aquafit ladies with their swimming caps—were now peering at your peen? What if you were already super self-conscious, being thirteen and not growing fast

145

enough and having seen the other guys in the dressing room at the hockey rink? What if you regularly measured yourself with a ruler? What if part of you deeply hated Jen but she looked so Neve Campbell from *Wild Things* that a larger part wanted her to laugh at your jokes and pat you on the chest the way she laughed-and-patted Drew after they hugged by the waterslide? What if you tried to adjust your trunks but you could see it was obvious and useless and you cursed your mother for buying this white and blue striped bathing suit and you could feel your cheeks going thermo-nuclear? What if you couldn't leave because Theo's mum was picking you up at five and you had no money or bus tickets and you didn't know the route home from Clayton Park anyway? Wouldn't you climb to the top of the five metre, thinking you'd do something megarad? Wouldn't you look down to make sure Jen and Tessa were watching and then half-run to the end of the platform, thinking swan dive, then thinking cannonball, then deciding on jackknife when it was already too late? What if you weren't totally sure what happened but you thought you slipped a bit and then you were in free-fall, totally crooked, arms churning air-butter? What if your side-shin hit first and then your ribs connected and all you could think of was those science class videos of sperm whales smacking their tales against the water? What if you stayed under as long as possible, just feeling that gigantic pain, worshipping it? What if when you came up you felt surprisingly not-that-bad and Jen and Tessa and the guys were all standing around laughing but this time they were laughing in a less mean way and when you hauled yourself onto the deck you stretched your arms towards the slanted pool roof, exposing a streak of purple-red water-rash down your whole right side, everyone started to cheer? What if Theo told you that was the gnarliest bellyflop of all time and Tessa chuckled and said "hilarious" and you decided right then that although her looks were subtler she was actually prettier than Jen?

This was how Gavin learned to cope. At some point in grade seven he realized he was never going to be the tallest or the handsomest or the most athletic. But the pool incident of the following December helped him to figure out that he could still be cool, still be liked.

How? Antics. What antics? Kid stuff. Funny stuff. Like enormous bellyflops. Like pushing over mailboxes. Like egging teachers' houses. Like writing "Tessa is Magnificent" in enormous letters on the gazebo at Ardmore Park. Like dropping an entire case of stink bombs through the window Mr. Aucoin the chain-smoking vice-principal left cracked in his Saturn. Like dry-humping mannequins in full public view at Sears. Like vandalizing the "Deaf Child" sign at the end of Theo's street so it read "Shush: Deaf Child." Like sack-mooning Theo's loserish former best friend Ted Clarke as he walked by Theo's window on the way home from his Warhammer league.

Gavin knew it was cheap and fragile. He knew he was a clown. But what else could he do? The world was rapidly splitting into those who laughed and those who were laughed at. He had to pick a side.

"Stand back!" Gavin shouted. "Big one. We're talking atomic."

He was on the couch at Theo's house, legs pitched in the air, lighter in hand. Theo's parents were split up and his mother, Nancy, was a navy engineer who spent her summer vacation reading thrillers in the backyard. Nancy wasn't around much on school days, so they went to Theo's place during lunch and after class.

Gavin sparked the flame and Drew and Theo jumped back, a gaseous blue stripe pealing through the room. Fartsound turned into butane-hiss and the boys went manic, shouting and snorting, their eyes welling up. Gavin rolled off the couch, plopping onto the floor and cackling as he clutched his butt: "I've been cauterized!"

Howling, Gavin headed to the upstairs bathroom. Checking himself in the mirror, he found that he was all right down there. On his way back downstairs, he passed Nancy's room.

What compelled him, that day, to look in? Clownish as he was, there were certain lines he usually wouldn't cross. Such as entering the bedroom of your friend's single mother, the one who is pretty with frazzled black hair and who compliments your sense of humour and encourages your song-writing even though Theo isn't supposed to show your lyrics to anyone. Such as glancing around the strange-smelling female space and honing in on the top dresser drawer, thinking whatever Nancy had in there might provide some code of entry into Tessa's heart. Such as opening that drawer and seeing a blue, tubular device and not knowing what it was at first and then thinking *no, it can't be*. Such as grabbing that device and racing downstairs and charging into the TV room waving it overhead.

"Dude." Drew said, squinting. "What the shit is that?"

Theo's face went parental. "What the hell, man?"

"I got it from Nancy's bedroom." Gavin held it up to his nose and sniffed hard. Then he pushed a button, made something whiz. "I call it *Blue Velvet*."

Drew laughed. "No way! Sick!"

"Gavin," Theo droned. "Put. That. Back."

Gavin spun, tube flailing in the air, its robotic head gyrating. "Put it back or I will hurt you."

Gavin danced over to Theo and shoved the whirring machine into his face. Theo sprung up but Gavin was already out of the room, feet thumping hardwood. A few grunts and thuds and he was out the front door, Theo close behind him.

The two boys raced down the street, sock feet slopping March slush. Gavin held the blue tube over his head, laughing and shouting, "Blue Velvet! Blue Velvet!"

They peeled around a few corners, deked a crew of grade sevens, and wheeled across Summit. A car slammed on the brakes and Gavin, entering Jackie Chan mode, leapt and slid over the hood, wagging his blue wand at the driver. With Theo's breath hot in his ear, Gavin got low and burst for the next corner.

Up ahead was the busy intersection across from the school. A string of cars was turning left and neither walk sign was on and just as Gavin was deciding what to do he felt hands on his shoulders, weight on his back. A lurch, and he was tumbling.

He landed palms-down in the snow-bank, watching the blue tube arc through the air. Theo's fists were thumping, searing into ribs and kidneys. The vibrator hit the pavement, cracked a little, and rolled under the tire of a minivan.

The light changed, and the van rolled forward.

Whenever the phone rang, Gavin went half psycho. He started coming home from school early, just so he could check the messages. Six weeks later, Nancy still hadn't called. Gavin's parents had no idea about the Blue Velvet incident. Part of Gavin wanted to write Nancy an apology letter. He craved some sort of penance, yearned to drain his guilt with words. But he was so used to the simple rhythm of either getting away with things or getting caught that he didn't know he could atone on his own. He thought discipline only came from the outside.

Every dream was a terror. One, in particular, kept recurring. He was in the principal's office, getting grilled by Mr. Aucoin. "What's this I hear about you parading around with a sex toy? I understand you're at an experimental age, but..." The dream always ended with Nancy showing up, bringing the smell of rain into the office with her. Mr. Aucoin would tell Gavin to apologize and he would try to say sorry but Nancy would always get a call on her cell and leave the room before he could get the words out. Then he'd be teetering on the edge of the five metre, trunks see-through, Aquafit ladies giggling, pool echo getting louder and louder. He'd look down and start to lose his footing. This time there was no water below. Reaching behind him, he would try to grab the platform but there was nothing there. Nothing but bleachy blue tiles rising towards him and the echoing laughter in his ears, almost deafening now.

Theo cooled off after a couple of weeks. Neither he nor Gavin could afford to stop hanging out with Drew, so they put up with each other. Before long they were back to their usual routine of weed smoking and mailbox dumping and pretending they weren't always pining about the same two or three girls. Months passed. Summer vacation started. Without really noticing, Gavin had a growth spurt. One of his mother's prettier friends said "you look so teenagerish" and he could not have asked for a better compliment. Drew told him he should probably start shaving unless he wanted a skivstash. The summer swelled and flexed. Gavin's social group multiplied, probably because he knew some girls who knew some older boys who knew how to get liquor.

Nancy still hadn't called.

Gavin found Theo and Drew at Ardmore, taking turns with a king-sized Sharpie. The marker oozed chemical hum as Theo scrawled his hideous tag, "Hellzbellz." The second zed curled down and sideways, stretching into a pitchfork.

Drew pumped Gavin's fist. "What's the word, Big Turd?"

"What's on, Small Dong?" Gavin reached into his backpack and pulled out a Gatorade bottle, two-thirds full of murky brown liquid.

"What's that?"

"Whiskey, rum, vodka. Splash of schnapps. I call it *Hybrid Vigour.*"

"Nasty."

Gavin took a long gulp. Gasping, he clutched his stomach, made a puke face, panted: "Fucking delicious."

Drew laughed, reaching for the bottle.

Soon their bellies were warm and toxic as they walked down to Westmount, chasing rumours of a field party. The August sun was setting on the far side of the field. Jen and Tessa were there with six or seven of their Cornwallis friends. There were also a few older kids from QE. Sam Hoffman handed a tall can to Gavin. Tessa was smoking a cigarette and he tried not to stare at her lips.

Soon Theo and the biggest Cornwallis dude were arm-wrestling and Drew was staggering around shouting "Hybrid Vigour!" Gavin was on his third beer and he'd had some drags of Tessa's cigarette and was starting to teeter on the far end of a buzz. He was trying to get closer to Tessa but Sam kept holding his shoulder and talking man-to-man.

When Sam loudly mentioned the electrical tower by the mall, Tessa leaned in, eyes sparkling. Sam said last year he was an arm's length from the top when the cops showed up and started pouring everyone's beer out. The cops were so stupid they just herded the kids out of there without ever looking up at the tower. When they were all gone, Sam climbed quietly down, a full bottle of citrus-flavoured vodka safe in his backpack.

"That's so cool," Tessa said. "We should do that tonight."

Sam shrugged. "I'm not getting stuck up there again."

"Whatever," Tessa said, looking around.

Gavin did not have it in him to spurn her curious eye.

When she saw him, gentle and plaintive and half-drunk, she beamed: "Gavin'll climb it."

Gavin laughed and shrugged and Sam slapped his back and soon they were all crowded around the electrical tower, everyone shouting Gavin's name. Drew yelled "Hybrid Vigour!" and Sam handed Gavin another tall can. He took a long drink and gave the beer to Tessa. She said she would guard it until the end of time and then she kissed him on the cheek and whispered "Good luck." Gavin started to climb.

At first it was nothing special: just climbing a ladder. The voices below got quieter and he wondered if the crowd was losing interest, but when he looked down he could see everyone huddled by the ladder, necks cranked back to watch. Tessa held the tall can up and wagged it at him like a trophy. He kept climbing.

Gavin could see cars pulling out of the West End Mall and the hill rising up from the Rotary, houses and streetlamps glowing. In the middle of it all was the Northwest Arm, cutting into the city, lights glittering off the wavering blackness of the inlet. Looking up, he saw that he was fifteen or twenty rungs from the top. He got eager, charged higher. Then he felt something strange. The air crackled and closed in around him. His arm hairs pricked. There was a chatter in his teeth, a buzz in his ears. He imagined himself standing on top of a huge blue whirring mountain.

Looking down, he saw Theo, Drew, and Tessa. They were all waving their arms frantically. They were so far away.

What if it was you, then, alone in the middle of the stark night sky, clinging to those shuddering rungs, hot terror searing like cobra venom? What if a dry panic clutched your throat and your bones went jittery and you both knew and didn't know what was going on? What if you heard that same pool echo from that day on the five metre but this time you knew it was just your own warbling ears? What if underneath the warble people were screaming and you were sure you recognized Tessa's Sarah Michelle Gellar-like voice trilling in the unthinkable distance? What if it was you, then, who looked out over the clouds and the stars and it was you who were in space and under water at the same time? What if there was a smell like burning hair and you saw the Aquafit ladies flying through the night sky, riding huge blue lightsabres and jabbing vibrating wands in your direction, and you couldn't tell if they were trying to save you or hurl you into an angry electric abyss? What if the charge was still building and all your muscles were twitching and the ladder was starting to char and every nerve and muscle was urging you to flee? What if the sky, then, turned unspeakably clear and lovely and the Aquafit angels were beckoning and a soft breeze soothed the burn and you were sure, for a moment, you could ride the wind? Wouldn't you dive towards the Northwest Arm, shooting for the glittering black pool? Wouldn't you think that maybe the cool water could save you, that once you landed safely Tessa would run down to the water, tearing off her clothes, and jump in beside you? Wouldn't you be astonished as you found yourself soaring not towards the Northwest Arm but straight for a leafy elm that made you think of Nancy reading in her shady backyard? Wouldn't you go reverential when, as some small branches broke your fall, you heard a voice lilting from the core of the tree, sounding just like Nancy, pleading for you to come closer? What would you do if when you landed between two large but merciful branches you heard that same silky voice saying you could forget all about Blue Velvet and the apology letter you never wrote? What if, as you lay there wheezing in the tree's embrace you ceased to wonder about life and death, ceased to pine over Tessa Brown? What if, when everything else was gone, you apologized and meant it and knew, knew with a feeling fiercer than truth, that Nancy understood?

SILICONE GIDDY

Yeah there were non-stop girls. Yeah the girls did not stop. Yeah we were silicone giddy. Yeah there were enhancements. Yeah there was tanned skin and colossal bass and buoyant handfuls of T&A. Yeah there were bright G-strings glowing in the blacklight. No you could not actually grab the buoyant handfuls of T&A without getting wrist-locked and possibly choke-slammed by the dragon-armed, lazy-eyed doorman and subsequently barred from this nirvana of non-stop girls. Yeah by dragon-armed I mean the doorman had badass dragons tattooed all over his enormous trisauraceps. Yeah there was sugar-free Red Bull. Yeah there was shitty coke laced with fuck knows. Yeah there was a shot called the Tequila Mockingbird. What else was there? A yoyo and an astronautical-themed room called the Space Heater that I was earnestly considering until I found out it cost two hundo just to walk in. A joint that may have had a hair in it, maybe something more sinister. A bride and groom who'd been married at noon, both of them grinding face into the stripper with blond streaks in her jet-black hair. At some point I learned the name of the stripper with blond streaks in her jet-black hair. Annie or Mandy or Bambi. Annamandambi. Also a white dude with a Jheri curl and a Vietnamese woman sipping straight well vodka and leering at Theo, one eye fluttering shut. A table full of chunky-watch-wearing Bobby Bigwheels who found out we were from Nova Scotia and started buying us Jäger bombs. Some sort of reparative gesture due to the endemic unemployment/poverty/alcoholism of Nova Scotia and Ontario's historic heist? When I told them I dropped some Jäger on a hamburger last year and created the Jäger bun they did not register the hilarity. At one point Theo walked into the dank strip-club kitchen—which had closed several hours earlier—and grabbed tiny, cold pulled pork sandwiches for the entire table. Drew invented a drink called the Comatose and Corrine countered with the Consensual Rufie. We proceeded to consensually rufie one another and then got into an argument about which sexual indiscretions should now be referred to as "pulling a Jian" in honour of J Ghomeshi. At some point the bartender cut Drew off and Drew tried to give him forty bucks for a pint but the bartender just wiggled his enormous neck muscles and said no. One of my last blustery memories is Drew wearing two pairs of wraparound sunglasses, shouting, "This bartender is a good bartender and a quality dude because I tried to bribe him and he would not accept the money!" Last call happened and Theo grabbed a suspiciously full pitcher off an empty table and poured us all pints and then the Bobby Bigwheels came back in from smoking cigarettes and asked where we got the now suspiciously empty pitcher and we said something about Jäger buns and walked off cackling into the vacuous lightscape of Yonge Street. Yeah there were non-stop girls. The marquee said so and the marquee was legit.

Why were we there? I don't mean the Silicone Palace. Should be obvious why we were there. I mean why tread the lurid urban cellulose of Yonge Street? Why were we milking the city's inflamed urethra when we might have been stumbling around Ossington or somewhere else genuinely cool? Why, even though I'd seen on Twitter that there were some good poets reading on Queen West, did I not go? I'll tell you why. Because I'm a half-closeted poet who becomes an inferno of envy every time I see a writer my age with a book out. Because I feel secretly threatened by tight-pants Torontonians with their slim bicycle wheels and I do my best to make jealousy and resentment seem like casual loathing due to Ontario's economic hegemony over the East. Because some part of me knows that to become a real writer I must become an adult and it is so much more fun to keep having a time and scribbling anonymous lines. Because me and Drew are two dirtbags spending two thirds of our lives cashing VLT chits in a dingy pub back home in Halifax and our tyrant boss would only give us two days off. Because even though my dad lives in Newmarket I'd rather share a room Drew booked in some mall-like downtown hotel than talk to my father about nine irons and search engine optimization and market segmentation. I'd rather listen to Drew fart and snore than listen to my father telling me he'll help me pay for an MBA if I want it but he won't help out with that cooking course at NSCC because that doesn't count as me vacating my comfort zone. Because after getting jagged in our hotel room and walking out the door the first thing we saw was a sign that said "non-stop girls" and although Corrine and Theo were saying about a place on Dundas it seemed safer and easier to get rowdy here than go somewhere dim and fashionable that would make me feel pathologically provincial.

But why were we in Toronto at all? Because Theo was finally marrying Corrine and we hadn't seen anything like enough of them since Corrine became a bona fide TDSB art teacher and Theo started his Ph.D. at York. Strange: this guy was going to be educating people about environmental studies and I remembered him tipping porta-potties as we walked home shittered from the Ward Room during that blur of beer and books I now call undergrad. I remembered how proud he was in grade ten when he traded a cigarette for a blowjob from Sarah "Darth Vader" MacDonald. I remembered him kicking out taillights because Handsome Pete whispered in his ear. I remembered him squealing the tires of his parents' VW as we peeled up Barrington Street, flying a skull and crossbones out the window. I remembered him convincing Drew to moon some girls from the back seat of said VW and then just easing on the brakes and coming to a gentle stop while Drew shrunk into an amoeba of embarrassment and it turned out the girls were Shelly and Tara from St. Pat's. I remembered him throwing an empty bottle of Colt Forty-Five high into the air, the glass skittering all over the skate park, each fragment a startled insect. That tall streetpunk shouting "my dog doesn't wear shoes!" and Theo just laughing, pitching another bottle into the floodlit sky. I remembered him getting in a fistfight with Drew the day we graduated high school because Drew thought it would be funny to kick a half-eaten McChicken out of Theo's hand. Drew kept saying he didn't want to fight but Theo was staggering and mouth-breathing into his face and eventually Drew just leaned back and one-punched him. Thankfully I caught him on the way down, because Theo weighed a solid two hundo back in the pre-vegetarian era and he was all white-socketed and wobble-kneed, tumbling tooth-first towards the phalt. For some reason Nancy still displays the picture on her mantelpiece: Theo wearing his tux and grinning next to Tara McDougle, one eye squeezed into a bloat of purple chub.

Which reminds me: Nancy.

Antsy Nancy. Anansi. Nance.

I might end up sitting at a table with Nancy. I will certainly see Nancy. I may well end up having to talk to Nancy. Sure it's been fifteen years since I stole Nance's vibrator, Blue Velvet, and tore around the neighbourhood before losing it to the tires of a moving van. Sure I never actually managed to apologize even though I've now formed at least eight million different syntactical combinations of the words I would have liked to say. Sure I've seen her hundreds of times since the Blue Velvet incident and it's always been, if anything, eerily congenial. Sure she's super respectable and in her mid-fifties now, though still miraculously mom-hot. Sure she's remarried to a doctor named Cliff who walks as if his genitals out-weigh a T-bone. Still: this awkwardness in me. This psychological kidney stone of shame. This complete cowardly inanity. I want nothing more than to cower before Nancy, bare the foul cavities of my soul and beg her forever-forgiveness. But that is something I will never do. That is something for which I do not have the marrow.

Theo and I are standing in line at a brunch place on Queen West and even if it was worth the wait my hangover would probably reject all gustatory value of the quail's eggs or cashew butter or whatever else makes Theo's favourite brunch spot so special. The line is a miasma of cut-off jean-shorts and Hitler Youth haircuts. There's a guy with a tangle of hops tattooed on his forearm, a beard that could nest an owl. A girl wearing a denim skirt is dribbling a basketball. Several dogs sit quietly about the outskirts of the patio, catching baguette ends and cubes of pancetta.

We are standing in line at a place that we may never get into and I am thinking of the vestibule of Dante's *Inferno*. I am thinking of the uncommitted, souls who chose neither goodness nor sin, the ones who sit on the shores of Acheron, perpetually stung by hornets and wasps, their existence a tailing pond. Nothing left but to envy the dead.

We are waiting, now, in this procession of hipster cred and I am thinking this place represents all the hollowness of Toronto and my dad is texting me to see if I want to go for brunch at Yonge and Eglinton and Theo is ranting about the Anthropocene. Theo is talking about the Anthropocene and how we're in the middle of the sixth mass extinction event in the last five hundred million years. I'm texting my dad to say thanks but no thanks and Theo's talking fracking and fossils and some geologist who believes that after humans go extinct the earth will be inherited by rats. "Look at their track record," he says. "A startlingly versatile genus. Even now they colonize and rule entire islands." I am nodding haphazardly and craving water, craving coffee, hankering to sit. Theo's talking *Rattus sanila* and *Rattus norvegicus* and saying how rats have been following humans around since the Pleistocene and there's a solid argument that the project of human civilization has built a perfect habitat for our whiskered successors. Once we're gone the rats could proliferate indefinitely, some growing as large as mastodons and others scrawling on the walls of caves.

We are finally sitting down and Theo is talking ocean acidification and river diversion and apparently human activity has transformed half the land mass of the planet and according to stratigraphers the changes taking place right now—radical carbon buildup and sudden polar melt—will be visible in the geological record a hundred million years into the future. It is this, Theo is saying as I order eggs Florentine, it is not music and pyramids and spaceships but pollution and massive scale destruction that will be humanity's real legacy.

I say that sounds kind of nice. There is a beauty about the idea. I like to think of the remnants, the traces of us meandering through the rock long after the species is gone. Our existence written into the skeleton of the planet, an arabesque signature on the scroll of deep time. A colossal, life-affirming gesture. A lost species shouting "We were here!" into unseen catacombs of the future.

"But what about short term?" I ask. "What about Nova Scotia?"

He says that by 2100 the sea level may rise six feet, which would be enough to basically drown Halifax. The good news is that with violent, unpredictable new storm systems moving north and rivers flooding all over, the oil economy may not even make it to 2100. "But basically," he says, "Halifax is a sinking peninsula." I am thinking that even this, in its way, is beautiful. My eggs Florentine arrives and it looks weary, the hollandaise suspiciously yellow. Maybe it was a mistake, learning to make my own hollandaise. Learning that it takes less than half an hour to turn toxic. I'm staring at an eggs Florentine, last night's IPA swirling in my guts, and I'm thinking about water, thinking about water and storms and sinking buildings. I'm thinking Venice, thinking Manhattan, thinking Halifax, imagining all these coastal cities a century from now—concrete pillars sprouting out of water, hives of algae and barnacles, the salt gnawing their walls and the current buckling their foundations. I see the tide creeping up over Citadel Hill, swallowing the old town clock and the ceremonial cannons. I picture the cobblestone walkway of Lower Water Street, entirely subsumed. What would it be like to swim my old neighbourhood, to dive down and see the underwater mailboxes and hydrants and parking lots, knowing each curve and corner of the ocean floor?

Theo and Corrine are getting married and I am thinking about hummus. Half-drunk, cogitating on hummus. How I've started to make my own hummus at home but I can never get it smooth enough. There are worse things to think about. I was thinking about Coeur de Pirate and the crone who breathes down my neck while I try to pour pints at the bar on Gottingen and now hummus. Hopefully there's hummus during cocktail hour. Fuck I love cocktail hour. And hummus. Theo's older cousin Rob the mediocre career musician is strumming shitty soft chords and I'm thinking about hummus. "Hummus," a waiter with braces once told me, is the Arabic word for chickpea but I always thought the word, in English, was strangely close to the word "human." Would it not be cute to name a child Hummus? Theo said the wedding food was going to be "gestacular," which he never would have said back in the when. Corrine, cool as she is, has somehow made Theo less cool, although I suppose he always was a bit of a granola-muncher at heart. Maybe there's only so much coolness, a quota available for any given couple. Otherwise they self-destruct, like Kurt and Courtney or Antony and Cleopatra. Or maybe I just haven't caught up with coolness as it aged. Maybe I need a recalibration. Are Theo and Corrine burgeoning yuppies or am I a burnout pushing thirty, recycling the same deadbeat charm that once made me semi-likeable? Oh, this ravage of perspectives.

Nancy smiles at me and I wave while trying not to acknowledge Cliff or look at Nancy's chest and I am thinking about the strippers from two nights ago. Thinking about that one with the double-string thong and the dimples on her back and the little silver balls pierced into those dimples. Thinking about her tenacious breasts. Small and sassy. An impertinent rack. She definitely had a thing for me. Body types: über compatible. My old best pal is getting married and I am thinking about stripper-patron body type compatibility. The sun is thumping as Theo stands at the head of the aisle and I am thinking about what STIs Miss Impertinent might be carrying and whether that is an unfair stereotype about strippers. Rob is picking up the volume as if to suggest Corrine is going to appear any moment and I am thinking I should probably drop the word "stripper" from my vocabulary and start calling them dancers. They are human beings after all. But could I still enjoy a wild night full of pulled pork sliders and Consensual Rufies among dancers?

A hush. Everyone stands. Enter bridesmaids.

"Hey, you're that guy, right?"

This from a cherub-faced redhead who's at least six four and I'm sure I knew back in the when though I can't remember where from. I have just decided that I loathe cocktail hour and I need another Tequila Mockingbird or whatever that grenadine-pink signature cocktail is called.

"You're going to have to specify."

"The guy who climbed that electrical tower. Gavin Something. That's you, right?"

"Sadly, yes."

"Woah. That was a big deal. Huge deal."

"Hot day huh?"

He looks confused. "Yeah." He chews his cocktail straw. "Beautiful."

A short girl who is far too attractive for Cherub Face shows up and suggests via arm language that she's Cherub Face's girlfriend. Just in case I'm about to scheme a move.

"Hey Babe," Cherub Face says. "Shazia, meet Gavin. He's the dude who got electrocuted in Halifax when I was in grade eleven. Climbed all the way to the top of a radio tower. He was a *Chronicle Herald* legend."

"Yep, that's me. Comical Harold."

The lanky cherub extends his freakishly large hand and decides to finally introduce himself as Rick Dingle and I'm remembering Ricky Dingle, Theo's gangly cousin who never took off his high-school basketball jacket and earned widespread acclaim for apparently copulating with three girls in one night at the "Safegrad" party at Harnish Farms. The last of these conquests on the roof of a barn in semi-full view of a gathering crowd of twenty plus.

"I was there that night at the tower," Dingle is saying. "I saw it all go down." Dingle sets his hands like he's holding a basketball and I know he's about to tell the story so I figure it's a good time to walk away. I grab two more Grenadine Dreams and head up to the treehouse. That's right, the venue has a treehouse which is far too huge and luxurious to be called a treehouse but is a mixture of tree and house no less. Although it's probably supposed to be for the kids Theo managed to reserve it for the groom's party and there are a few guitars up there and hopefully a stash of whiskey and as I climb the stairs I can see that it's enticingly desolate.

I open the door onto fake hunting gear and fake fireplace and ersatz bearskin. The room is ringed with sauna-style wooden benches and on one of them, all alone, sits Corrine, nursing a Nuclear Sunbeam, shoes kicked onto the floor.

"Shit. Hey Corrine. I thought this was, like, the man cave."

She shrugs. "The woman cave is full of mothers going menopausal."

"What? But you're married now. I thought that ended when you said 'till death rend us asunder.'"

"Yeah no. Menopause still happens."

"Bummer," I say, laughing and thinking this is why I am still fond of Corrine in spite of all the history, thinking that if Dante's Brunch Vestibule represents everything that is loathsome about Toronto then Corrine is everything exciting and genuine about this place.

We remain silent for a while, her sitting, me standing, both sipping rosy-hued consolation. The treehouse smells like cheap scotch and rented suits.

"The other night was fun, huh?"

"Possibly too fun?" I sit down beside her.

"That one stripper, Sandy? Total smokeshow. Blond streaks in her jet-black hair?"

"You mean Bambi? She was into me."

Corrine eyes me over her Saccharine Sunset.

"I'm talking contact. Serious contact."

"Reluctant eye contact? What'd she charge for that?"

We laugh. When our voices peter we can hear the babble of pleasantries below.

"So. Congratulations." I am serious and yet it is hard not to roll my eyes. I offer my glass and clink, then sip. "Beautiful ceremony and all that."

"Yes," she stiffens her back, voice going suburban. "Lovely. Such a beautiful bride."

We laugh together again. "Not bad," I admit. "Theo's a lucky dude."

She keeps her body still, eyes on the floor. Her shoulders say *don't go there*. Her mouth says, "How's the poetry going?"

I gulp the rest of my Wet Dreamsicle.

"Good, I'm thinking of putting a manuscript together."

"Published anything lately?"

"Yeah, here and there."

"Email me. I'd love to see some new work."

I watch the ice melt in my empty glass and hope that Corrine is not going to ask me again about the thing with her friend Lara and then she asks me again about the thing with her friend Lara. Cute Lara with the bust of Shelly tattooed on her shoulder above Plath's yew tree. Lara who couldn't make it tonight because her second book is launching in Vancouver. Corrine is saying once again about Lara's new online literary journal, as if I didn't already know all about Lara Barryman's found poetry and *Samizdat*'s mandate to publish mixed media and digital poetry projects. Corrine is saying Lara recently got some huge amount of funding and she's looking for people, saying nothing too lucrative, saying foot in the door, saying crash on her and Theo's couch for a month or two. I am thinking no and thinking why do you want to help me and saying sounds cool, saying I'll think about it. Corrine says please do and then stays quiet for a while. Finally she blurts out that Theo really admires and envies me and there is an eerily timed cheer from below and I ask what for and she says for staying in Halifax. "He's always respected you," she says. "He misses you and wishes he could've stayed there too. It's hard for him you know?" I'm thinking bullshit and thinking why are you trying to get me to move here but also thinking maybe if I came Theo and I could really reconnect. Maybe I could date Lara or one of her friends and become *Samizdat*'s associate editor and get a nepotistic but who cares if its nepotistic book deal.

I hear a glass smashing somewhere outside and look up to see Drew and Theo swaggering up to the treehouse. Drew looks to be prematurely hammered, finishing a cigarette and talking loudly with an arm around Theo.

Corrine stands up. "Well, I guess I should show my face down below."

I nod. "Gobble 'em up, Bridezilla."

She pauses, stepping into a shoe. "What do you think of Theo's aunt Vanessa?"

Vanessa? As in Nancy's little sister. As in coolest aunt ever. As in married to a pro snowboarder for fifteen years and said marriage recently ended, possibly because Vanessa put on weight though still looks great. As in used to do liquor runs when we were fifteen as long as we'd share the beer with her and tell her about the cool new music even though we didn't know shit about the cool new music and just listened to the same DayGlo CDs over and over. As in rockabilly-red hair and full sleeves of pin-up girls and skeletons and generally rad tattoos. As in basically the reason I took up snowboarding at fourteen was to one day go pro and pull a corked ten-eighty while stealing her from her balding mediocre pro husband. As in many many indecent nights with the duvet fluttering as my breathing increased.

"She's cool. Why?"

Corrine shrugs. "Says you turned suddenly handsome at twenty-five and now you're fully bangable." Does Corrine really think it's funny or cool to say something like this as she's walking away?

Drew stumbles into the treehouse as Corrine and Theo pause to kiss. "Bra!" Drew high-fives me. "What are you doing up here, composing some poetry?" Drew does ghouly fingers every time he says the word "poetry." Chuckling, he reaches into the faux-fireplace and finds his stash of Johnny black. He takes a swill from the bottle and holds it up with two hands like some tiny rectangular Stanley Cup. And then he is humping treehouse air and slurring, "Good to know you're still pounding like Ezra." As he hands me the bottle of JWB I am thinking of Vanessa. I am swilling whiskey and thinking of Vanessa, thinking of Vanessa, thinking of Lara and *Samizdat*, thinking of Corrine thinking of Nancy.

Is there history with Corrine? When is there not history? We all met Corrine back in the when. She'd moved to Halifax because her father had a visiting professorship at Dalhousie. She showed up at the Bowl with some streetpunks she'd met on Spring Garden, wearing a plaid skirt with torn fishnets and looking for pot. All of us middle class white boys in studded leather jackets were racing to roll up and give her supers. We were sixteen, all virgins, and thought people from Moncton were exotic. She was eighteen from a land of streetcars and Sky Domes, all tattoos and GG Allin raunch, her body a swirling fantasia. She was reading Marx's notebooks and when I said I was an anarchist she asked "collectivist or individualist?," which left me stammering and smitten.

Drew, Theo, and I were all besotted and I'm still baffled that I got to be the first to date her. Six atomic months and then intensities faded. Lethargy happened. Too much pot happened. A twenty-five-year-old metal drummer with a three-foot beard happened. Promising we'd always be friends and meaning I would secretly always want to get back together happened. Then university and a few sporadic girlfriends happened and some version of the question "what are you doing with your life?" or the word "career" happened and always wondering what could have happened with Corrine happened. And that is basically my entire romantic history. Do I care much now? Of course not. Have I forgotten utterly and forgiven entirely? Of course I have. Am I finally able at this point to appreciate her company as a friend, sans jealousy? Naturally. Do I sometimes fondly recall the tattoos that only myself and a select ten or fifteen others have ever witnessed? Very rarely. Do I periodically indulge in recollections of the time I emailed her my experiments with imagism and she wrote back that she liked the way the language sounded like a bright and tortured music? Never. Did the thing that she said next—*there is a real voice in you, struggling to break through*—become an anthem for all my deepest hopes and desolations? Categorically not.

Break, voice. Dissolve these paltry surfaces.

Unfurl exalted, devastate the vast.

Vanessa's tossing me shameless eyeballs but I keep glancing at Nancy's legs, having, as I happen to have, a clear view of Nancy's mumazing thighs which she seems to think are concealed by the table cloth. Several times throughout dinner Cliff has reached down for a healthy inner thigh rub which makes me feel kind of hot and also pervier than usual. The couple next to me at the table—one of Theo's friends from environmental studs with a white girl wearing a sari—keep kissing and talking about how much better than this their wedding is going to be. Corrine's father Anthony the classics professor is monotoning away, saying how marriage is a contract, saying Hegel this and Rousseau that and I'm seriously considering a nap if I don't get another non-red-wine beverage in me ASAP and then I get some mating season eye contact from Vanessa and I'm thinking why not as the server puts crème brûlée down in front of me. I'm taking a spoonful of crème brûlée and thinking where the hell is my coffee and if I ever get married I will serve Irish coffee for dessert and why not move to Toronto and get a part-time job copy-editing for *Samizdat*? Why not make a run for Vanessa? Why the shit not?

Our births, our deaths, our dearest traumas. What important events of our lives do not take place in the hospital? It was in the hospital that I returned to quasi-life a few days after I got drunk, climbed an electrical tower, and peeled through the night sky into the tree that saved me. Theo came to the hospital one of the first days I was well enough to accept visitors. He said he was sorry he let me do it and I said he should be sorry. I said he should go back and climb the tower himself. I lifted the blanket to show him the bandages—all the way up my left side. "Talk to me when you've got a set to match," I said, turning to face the wall. But he didn't leave. He took my hand and squeezed it, forgetting all the panicked fears of a fourteen-year-old boy and just holding me. We didn't cry or say anything but at that moment he was my brother and my father and my mother and my child.

Gavin is standing in the single-person unisex washroom at his best friend's wedding and the toilet won't flush. He is idiotically pressing the lever a second time and of course the water only rises higher, spins its lethargic indolent spin. The water seems, almost, to snarl. Little blobs of shame swirling in the strange current of that lazy but unstoppable cyclone. Someone—presumably a delicate beauty in a brilliant velour dress—gently knuckles the door. Gavin tries to bark but instead begs "just a minute," hyper-aware of the five or six people standing in line, including Corrine's Estonian cousin, the one he'd lamely flirted with until they ran out of shared language. Gavin is looking for a plunger, desperate for a plunger and finding none and the water is rising, the water is not going down even as he waits and waits and resists the urge to flush again. A sleek sheet of water sluices over the porcelain coping and slicks down onto the tile and Gavin knows that flushing again is the absolute wrong thing to do but here he is with the mire of him, the very filth of him cresting the toilet's lip. Does he coat his palms in paper towel and grab that raw human waste and fling it into the trash before washing his hands manically in the small beaded-glass sink with the stone garden about the lovely drain? Or does he walk out barking outrage and saying sorry folks, crafting a makeshift

"Out of Order" sign from an old pack of cigarettes before stomping off to inform management? Or does he stand there indefinitely with his finger hovering on the lever, his mind hissing alternately *push push don't you fucking dare push* and the beautiful Estonian with her lovely tanned plenty whispering through the door that it is getting urgent? Does he stand there motionless with his finger on the lever and all that rank waste rising unstoppable, rising slow?

I have lived 5,512 days since that night and never has the moon set without my giving some reflection to it. And why have I counted the number of days? Because I almost died, I suppose. But, more than that, because when I woke up in the hospital I realized that not only did I almost die but if I *had* died it would not have made any difference to anything or anyone. I realized, then, that I was virtually alone in this heaving gasp of a cosmos. That I was helpless against the colossal indifference where space meets time and that not even soaring through the air, not even a bolt of lightning shuddering my teenage body could save me or heal me or make me into something that mattered. And maybe the electricity that scorched my flesh gave me my voice, my real voice. But it also kept that voice from breaking through.

I reflect on this now from the treehouse, where I am waiting for Vanessa. I returned her gaze and nodded up to the treehouse and sauntered outside, looking over my shoulder to make sure she saw. The bright half moon and the cool night air blasted me into temporary sobriety. I climbed the steps slowly and walked into the treehouse, sensing through the darkness the empty cocktail glasses and the smell of wood and sweat. My fingers paused on the light switch for a moment, gently fondling the plastic nub. Then I decided no and left the lights out. I sat down on the hard wooden bench and listened to the echo of speeches sprawling into the courtyard and rising up through the floorboards. Now Theo is speaking and the laughter is coming fast and easy. He always was an articulate bastard. Should I feel bad for missing his speech? Maybe, but I feel more able to love him up here, just hearing the sound of his voice in the distance, unable to parse the words.

Stop right now, thank you very much. The DJ is playing Spice Girls and Corrine's friends are bobbing joyfully around the dance floor. They know all the words and all the choreography. *I need somebody with the human touch.* Sari Girl is gyrating in front of the Environmental Stud, dipping ludicrously close to the floor. The Environmental Stud is doing tight Travolta arm-circles. A handsome man with a close-trimmed beard is dancing with Vanessa, who is getting shattered in a hurry. She never came to me in the treehouse and now I'm wondering if she really looked at me across the dining room. Could Corrine have made up the whole "bangable" thing?

The only answer to such questions is hard liquor so Drew and I lean on the bar, doing Malt Whitmans, doing JD Salingers, doing Gertrude Steins. Before long Drew goes full bellige, yelling that he is the mayor of the wedding, yelling that he is MC Hammered. Theo comes by and we tell him he'd better talk to the DJ and he says we might want to slow down because it's just past nine. I make the responsible choice and ask the barkeep for two Caesars and he hands me two waters and says "trust me." The Spice Girls fade into Backstreet Boys and somehow Drew and me are on the dance floor, doing the zombie dance and screaming out the words to "Backstreet's Back." Vanessa approaches and leans in to say something and her lips brush against my neck and I laugh, pretending I can hear her, then grab her arm as Queen comes on. Then it's Bowie then Madonna then "Little Red Corvette" and then I have to go to the bathroom and when I come outside Vanessa lifts up her dress and flashes me her butt and it is genuinely not bad, even though she is wearing a total stepmom thong. She pulls me outside and we fall, giggling, into some bushes and as far as I can tell we are actually having sex but I'm too wasted to feel much and then Drew and Ricky Dingle come outside and apparently they don't see us because they light cigarettes like ten feet away so we stop having numb sex and just lie there, giggling. Someone shines an iPhone flashlight on us and then Vanessa's up and running away and I don't know if I should follow her but I'm getting a gnarly case of the spins lying here in the soil looking up at the stars.

That angelic asshole Dingle helps me up and drags me inside and gets me a bottle of water. I slouch at the table, trying to stitch my consciousness together one sense at a time, struggling against the spinning lights on the dance floor. I check my phone and see three texts from my dad, the last of which reads "Drinkypoos?" I put my phone away without responding, wondering whether I'm really going to fly home tomorrow afternoon without seeing my father at all and whether that is a time issue or some seriously twisted attempt at revenge.

The music switches to a slow song which means blaring lightshow torture melts into disco ball swirl. Corrine dances with her father and Theo comes and sits down with me and asks how I'm doing and do I need something. I say fine and yes I need someone to love me unconditionally for the rest of my life. He laughs and says I should consider getting a dog and then somehow produces a slice of wedding cake and a lukewarm coffee and I mouw the cake and sip the coffee and say actually a dog is not a bad idea.

He makes small talk until the food and coffee sobers me up and then asks if I've ever considered leaving town, says that for a lot of people leaving home is the only way to find their path. I tell him maybe I don't want the same success he does. Maybe I'm happy just to work my day job and write my poems and hang out with Drew and the rest of the boys in Halifax because I can't imagine better friends or a better place. He nods and smiles and seems to not quite believe me and in fact I'm not sure how much I believe myself. Of course I know that my friends who've left the province all have careers or partners or exotic travel stories and I have none of these things. Of course I know that on some level this place is like a succubus. A leech feeding, almost imperceptibly, on the future.

"You know I love Halifax as much as you do," he says eventually.

"Yeah, well, it's easier to love something from a distance."

"You think it's easy?" Theo barks. "You think I wanted to leave? No. I miss you and I miss my mother and I think of the ocean every night as I fall asleep. I have a deep respect for your choice to stay. But I was stagnating there, and at some point I had to grow up. I don't know if it's that peninsula or that city or just our particular group of privileged Haligonians but I know that our friends who stay home are stagnating. Treading water on a sinking peninsula. But I also know I love that sinking peninsula more than anything else. That that is the tension that I live in every day. The tension that I am."

I nod and say I think I know what he means. I do not say that I am living the other side of that tension, always wondering what it might mean to move to Toronto and take my father's offer of the Newmarket basement until I get settled. I do not say about living one's whole life keeping one eye trained on the metropole, do not mention what he already knows: that my Nova Scotian father left me and my Nova Scotian mother for Ontario when I was ten years old and how it feels like acid searing flesh that my now-rich father clearly thinks this is the best decision he ever made. I do not say that that is a version of the tension shaping basically all young Nova Scotians I know: to leave and thrive or stay and suffer.

Suffer economically but maybe not spiritually. Suffer and feel in the place you want to be.

We sit there for a while in silence, watching Corrine slow dance with one of her uncles. After a while Theo blurts that he's sorry. He didn't mean to let everything slip out like that but it's just he's a bit drunk and he worries about me and he wants to see me do well by myself and we're almost thirty now and sometimes he gets a little emotional.

I tell him I'm sorry too and maybe he's right and he takes my hand and squeezes it. A server comes around and tops up my coffee and I sit there staring into the cup until Theo says it's okay. I ask what's okay and he says, "The whole history. You and Corrine. It's in the past and it's okay and I'm sorry about that too." I'm thinking maybe it's not effing okay for me and I didn't ask for Theo's infuriating forgiveness but I know he means well so I put my hand on his shoulder and say, "Thank you, thank you, let's just forget about the rest of it. All that matters right now is that I am so happy for the two of you and she looks magnificent."

Theo hugs me and says thanks and then the DJ leaves for an interlude that Theo seems to know about because he gets up and goes to stand by Corrine as Rob takes the stage and starts to play a horrendous acoustic version of "Purple Rain." I nurse my coffee and listen to Rob's falsetto and imagine the kinds of dog I could get and picture a new Gavin, one who exercises three times a week and writes poetry every morning and eats kale and quinoa and meets all kinds of wholesome women at the dog park, a Gavin who starts thinking of adult human females as women instead of strippers or dancers or girls. It turns out that miraculously enough there are more speeches and Drew of all people is giving a speech and when he says "Theo and Corrine, you guys are as close to my heart as my heart is to my body" I stand up and applaud uproariously and walk outside, thinking treehouse. Maybe I'll find my dog in the treehouse.

I pass the bathroom and there's a crowd and some commotion and I gather that Vanessa's in there and someone hisses "what did you do to her?" and I keep walking, thinking treehouse, thinking quinoa, definitely not thinking Corrine Lara Corrine Nancy and then outside in the courtyard on the way to the treehouse I see Nancy, see her alone for the first time tonight, and I know there is only one thing it could mean.

Theo came to visit, but Nancy never did. I spent two more weeks in the Victoria General and then went through months of bedrest at home. The doctors said I was lucky to be alive. As if we aren't all lucky to be alive. But me especially, I guess. I had come ridiculously close to death and it took more than a decade before I started to feel unrattled by that. My dad came down from Ontario for a week and as usual he had nothing to discuss except sampling variables and regional demographics. It just made it weird between him and my mother, who didn't know what to do except ensure I took my medications and rubbed the right creams on the right places. It was probably stupid and strange but I always imagined that Nancy would show up for a visit. I really thought that the touch of her hands could heal the burns. I thought that Nancy could peel back the bandages and lay her palms on my chapped white flesh and make me pink and bright and clean, make me a child again.

I wonder where she's coming from but I don't think too hard about it and as she tries to walk straight past me with a politely motherish smile I stand in front of her and say "Hello Nancy" in a tone that I hope means "Nancy you have to stop here and talk to me now because you're the only person who can save me" and somehow it works and she stops. And then I'm wondering what I need to be saved from and it's not quite the dive bar and it's not quite the underemployed malaise of Nova Scotia because in some weird way I love both those things.

Nancy is wearing a black dress with spaghetti straps and I'm looking at the brown curve of her shoulders, tanned from the hours reading thrillers in her yard. There are freckles all over them, a thousand tiny brown droplets melting into the butter of her skin. The backs of her arms are taut, firmed by hours of impeccable Phalakasana. But this is not about any of that. This is not about the fact that she has aged like a sunset. This is about salvation.

I'm thinking maybe what I need to be saved from is that toxic shame in me, the shame that I can't quite locate but is of course about more than stealing Blue Velvet back in the when. But as I peer into the creamy galaxies of Nancy's shoulders and think about putting a hand on her sun-browned neck I realize there will be no forgiveness of this shame because the shame is me. It is the shame of coming from a colonial, sinking, backwater peninsula. The shame of being descended from a heinous mixture of the British and French settlers who stole that place from the Mi'kmaq and built cannons and burnt villages and then sold the whole package to Canada. But more than that the shame is the shame of everything I've ever done and felt and fucked and wanted and repressed. The shame is basic human depravity and it is howling, howling through me now.

I'm thinking maybe I don't need to be saved, just salved, and I'm saying "Nancy, Nancy I'm sorry" and she is laughing nervously and saying sorry for what and asking me where's Vanessa and I'm saying "no no seriously I'm sorry."

Enter silence. Enter gravitas.

The night peals into outer space and the courtyard becomes a vacuum.

Nancy looks at me with genuine concern and I say, "I'm sorry about Blue Velvet. About your, well, sex toy, and everything."

Enter harrowing, harrowing moments.

I am an astronaut drifting away from a spaceship and all the fuel expired.

Nancy is not laughing now. "It's okay, Gavin, it's in the past. But thank you."

She moves to walk away but I reach out for her and she flinches and gives me an are-you-fucking-serious look and then actually says "are you fucking serious?" I say "I think I am fucking serious" and "I've always sort of loved you" and "save me." Then I lean down to kiss her and she's whispering *not here*, hissing *let's go up to the treehouse*, but then she's actually saying, "Gavin, don't be ridiculous." I try to kiss her again, thinking maybe if she just slapped me but she doesn't just slap me, she backs away again and says "No" in a way that is unequivocal. She puts her hand on my shoulder and says, "Don't be ridiculous. I can't save you, Gavin. I will never be able to save you. I don't know what's wrong and I'm sure it's hard but I will never be able to save you." Nancy walks back inside and I am alone in the darkness.

Floating, floating, in the darkness of the courtyard at the end of the known.

I wait as long as I can, listening to the bass thud and the girls squealing "It's my song!" every three minutes. Then I go inside to find Vanessa but the chorus of bridesmaids outside the ladies' informs me that she's still incapacitated and it's still my fault and I'm thinking maybe it's good that I didn't have to fully deflate that particular balloon of my horny adolescent imaginary. Or maybe that fantasy is already looking like a well-trod condom strewn across a grungy sidewalk.

I go to the bar and am surprised to find Drew neither there nor on the dancefloor. I don't see Theo or Corrine either and the bartender tells me it's last call so I get two beers and a bottle of water and walk away.

Back in the courtyard I hear voices coming from the treehouse. I ascend the stairs and hear the sound of acoustic guitars. Drew and Theo are strumming fast power chords and they both send me huge grins as I walk in. They are playing The Misfits, playing GG Allin, the songs we used to play back in the when. And I'm thinking who cares that the DJ is playing Miley Cyrus and who cares that I sent twenty poems out last year and only one got published and who cares that I work at a dive bar with an undergrad degree in English and philosophy wilting in my back pocket and who cares that Vanessa is hugging a toilet and who cares that although Nancy says she forgives me for the Blue Velvet thing I will never feel forgiven for the shame that has made me? Who cares? I am here and I am alive. I am thinking maybe I will go to cooking school and start a catering company, perfect that walnut-mushroom burger, that artisanal ginger ketchup. I am thinking I will get a dog, put together a book of poetry, sign up for OkCupid because people my age don't meet at the bar. I am thinking what I have known all along: that I will not move here, will not work for *Samizdat*, will not date Lara or schmooze Torontonian because I could never write properly about bike lanes and brunch lines and the trees that grow in condo gardens.

I stumble out onto the porch and Theo and Drew and Corrine follow me. Theo has some cigars and we light them and then I put my arms around them all at once and we are alive, here, together. One Upper Canadian princess and three children of a stolen ocean standing in a tree, looking out through the branches at the city and the night sky, living. When I get home I will dive head-first into the cold water of the North Atlantic. I will feel the sand saturating the water as it kicks back from the surf. The sea will rub the sand against my body like softest pestle, grinding the mortar of me, and I will be happy and moving and tortured and alive. Because if this peninsula is going to sink, I am going to sink with it.

Sink gentle, sink wild, sink triumphal.

Sink weightless, weightless in the womb-dark deep.

SUTURE

Imagine it's you facing the loss of the still-ripening cherries between your legs. Imagine you're the black-and-white splotched Jack Russel mix with a knuckle in your tail from getting run over by a mountain bike. Imagine you have no idea that a vet might soon be opening your scrotal sac and scraping out your testes and your vas deferens like a chef spooning seeds from a cantaloupe. Imagine you have to wear a cone on your head to keep you from licking your own stitched and scabby genital region. A cone to stop you from sniffing and tonguing the sore and pungent spots you desperately want to tongue and sniff. Because tonguing is how you treat your wounds, sniffing how you sculpt your world. Picture these humans you desperately adore, the male with the scars and the female with different coloured eyes. Conjure these companions who walk city streets stooping to collect your steaming excretions in winter chill, handling the warmth of your digested kibble through the coarse and rustling plastic of a poo bag. These people who nuzzle and spoon you, who snoog you softly in their beds at night. Who named you Ezra but mostly call you Chèvre and Bedrock and Nebuchadnezzra. Who cook chicken necks to mix with your food, placing those gizzards in a special Tupperware marked "dog chicken." Microwaving that rangy poultry for fifteen seconds to take off the chill before mixing it with your grain-free kibble. These people who refuse to eat meat themselves but who care enough about your health and pleasure to bring chicken necks into their kitchen. Now imagine that these same people decide to remove your genitals. Because your dispatched testes mean an easier life for them. Mean not having to show face at the dog park and say "intact." Because this way all your erotic drives can be channelled into puppy playdates and doggy daycares and vigorous Kong-tossing sessions. Imagine that these people who call themselves animal lovers want to reroute your sexuality, to sluice your eros—to make every light in you beam for them and them alone.

This is the quiet perversity looping through Gavin's mind as he watches Rubix drop a drool-slathered frisbee at his feet. This is the societal hypocrisy that has caused the first real disagreement between Gavin and Zara.

Zara. The vegan with optic heterochromia who works the counter at the neighbourhood microbrew and volunteers at the Ecology Network. Zara who was born in Mumbai and has never been back but has vowed to take Gavin there one day to watch cricket and swim with sea turtles and sip tea under whispering fronds. Zara who did not turn Gavin's life around but pushed it into a delirious cartwheel of pleasure and something larger. Zara who said yes he should go to cooking school at NSCC and no he was not too old to start a new career. Zara who read his chapbook of poems about teeth decomposing in Coke cans and said she liked their gothic ecstasies, said they read like the music of blood-drunk mosquitoes and what better compliment could she have given? Zara with one blue eye and one green and Gavin never able to say which was more ravishing against the opiate dusk of her skin. Zara the woman who is adamant about the benefits of neutering their dog.

Gavin stoops to grab that drool-slick disc as Hermione the red-coated duck toller takes a vigorous interest in Ezra's crotch. He tosses the frisbee and watches Rubix blast across the pitch while Hermione continues to sniff Ezra's privates, tail thwacking Gavin's shins. Gavin knows Hermione was spayed last April but still he follows protocol—tugs Ezra away and tells Hermione's person that Ezra hasn't been neutered yet, prompting a grimace from that toqued barista. Kijiji trees a squirrel and Ezra charges over to howl up at the quivering tuft of russet. Gavin watches Ezra leap at the tree, watches that gangly puppy coil and spring and wonders how it happened—when did such joy become available through a body other than his own?

Zara is home brewing peppermint tea and as they say hello he wills the glow of this woman standing over the stove they share to seep through him. She pecks his cheek and he says he missed her and they embrace like nothing is wrong. She pours him tea and puts peanut butter in a Kong for Ezra. Much as he wants everything to be resolved between them Gavin finds himself saying about Hermione's person. Saying who does she think she is and all this bourgeois nuclear dog family bullshit. Zara scoffs and they glitch into the argument that has come to define them. Gavin says about the banality, says it is just so perverse to have this nation of so-called pet lovers scraping out their companion animals like Halloween pumpkins.

Zara mentions the safety, the docility, the trainability.

They throw cancers back and forth.

Gavin adds weight gain, surgery complications, the cone.

"Would you feel the same if it was a female?"

"Of course," Gavin lies. He has weighed this question many times and remains deeply, shamefully unsure.

"How much of your life are you willing to spend on these same words, this same conversation?"

"A lot, I hope." He tries to be cute but sounds petulant. Meaning Zara heads to the bathroom to take a triumphant shower. Gavin picks up his collected Baudelaire and stares at a poem for a long time, not turning the page. Zara sings a Springsteen tune into the shower head and the notes come to Gavin thick and muddled through the bathroom wall.

They were sixteen and they'd set out swimming in the harbour—Theo and Gavin and Drew. Sixteen and swimming in that sewage-slick elbow of the Atlantic and they knew it wasn't safe but the mushrooms did not care for prohibitions, did not fear bacteria, did not respect sanitation. Swimming among the tiny jellyfish and the tampon applicators, among the unrecorded suicides and the debris of 1917. They'd set out together but soon they were alone, each boy on his own journey through water and body and mind. Drew and Theo disappeared and Gavin was not concerned with them. The water moved over him and each slither was an undreamt dermal rhapsody. He swam through the black, swam beneath the surface and found to his pleasure that he had no need for air. Through the darkness he saw a hulking shadow, gnarled and round.

Gavin and Zara met on a rideshare to Montreal. He'd borrowed his mother's car to go to there for the launch of his poetry chapbook, *Agricola Dentata*, and he didn't want to do the twelve-hour drive alone. His ad got a few responses and of course he chose the woman's name and when she climbed in the car wearing a romper that showed the floral tattoos stitched up her thighs he felt sleazy and fearful and awed. There was traffic on Robie Street and Gavin brought up the city's need for light rail but Zara said that was what she loved about the place, that they were stuck on this peninsula within a peninsula so the city couldn't possibly get any bigger. He said she was right, said the only way to build was up but the people wouldn't abide that because they didn't want to ruin the view from Citadel Hill.

"Fucking perfect!" she laughed. "This place is so brilliantly backward."

Zara was from Halifax and had gone to St. Pats while Gavin went to QE. She was only a year younger but they somehow knew none of the same people—she'd been in French immersion and the high school musical while he was drinking Colt Forty-Five and skateboarding poorly and secretly writing blankverse sonnets about fingernail clippings.

Dropping her in Mile End he wanted to ask for her number but only managed to blurt about the poetry launch. She said "that could be cool" and slid out of the car and he assumed he'd never see her again until he was two poems deep in the dark room full of hostile strangers. She strode in with her shoulder bandaged from a fresh tattoo and laughed with the bartender in the middle of his poem. Laughed and flicked back her hair and became a streak of neon in a sepia photo. After his set he bought her a cider and as they chatted their mouths and knees drew closer and closer. When he went to the bathroom she crept up behind him at the sink and hissed "whatever you want" into his neck but another poet walked in and they stumbled out giggling.

They met Zara's friends at a dangerously packed bar on the Plateau. Zara found a storeroom and thieved two six packs of Stella, stashing the beer in the corner where the two of them kissed and rubbed thighs and drank free until close. They stumbled home with five or six of Zara's Blundstone-wearing girlfriends, all of whom were vocally unimpressed by Gavin's skate shoes and straight-leg jeans. Gavin peed in an alley and got a ticket from a police officer in camo shorts and when he looked up Zara and her friends were gone.

He drove home the next day hungover and cursing himself for not getting her number. Lying in his bed in Halifax he told himself not to but finally got up at three in the morning and emailed her. She wrote back a single, unpunctuated line—"what's your address?" Three days later she showed up with a growler of IPA and a toothbrush and she hadn't left since.

Gavin goes for post-work drinks with Theo and Drew, who won't stop swiping his phone. Drew is bragging that he never swipes left and using words like "Tinderella" and Gavin is wondering how this culture can believe it is the dogs of the world who need their sexuality adjusted. Gavin starts a conversation about turning thirty, how people suddenly stop looking at you as if you were always about to throw a stink bomb. Drew says girls love thirty-year-old guys and points to the grey streak in his lumberjack beard and Gavin can't tell how serious he is. Theo snorts but he is not there, he has drifted. He's been euphoric since Corrine got a job at Halifax Grammar and they moved back to town but tonight he seems punctured. He says something about how we're all nothing but deteriorating bodies and the comment looms in the acrid bar air.

They order tequilas and Gavin asks the waiter for a lemon. Drew scoffs "training wheels" and Gavin thinks as he often has about how dogs are like practise children. All the thirty-ish couples he knows who didn't want or couldn't afford or couldn't commit to human children got dogs instead, their nurturing instincts channelled into doggy daycares and doggy spas and doggy treats. Gavin thinks that a dog might be better than a kid anyway because it never grows up, never turns teenage and gets caught shoplifting. Never totals the car. A dog never winds up staggering across streets heedless of lights and horns and intersections, face scaled with meth sores.

But dogs come with their own set of problems. Such as the one facing him now as these three old friends sit together ignoring each other at a table. Three faces lit by the ionic cosmos of Drew's phone. Gavin is considering how silence is alright between old friends, how silence between long-time pals is even kind of pleasant, when Theo blurts the news about his mother. No warning whatever and then the words "early onset" and Drew and Gavin sitting there in the dark, gulping. Drew asks how could this have happened and Theo shrugs and downs his beer and Gavin finds himself saying it's okay. Saying it's okay and not believing it and thinking of Nancy, cosmic Nancy, her tanned calves in platform sandals just two summers ago at Theo's wedding. How could a body that sleek and sure ever break down? He is thinking of Nancy in all her ageless splendour and putting a hand on Theo's shoulder and saying it will be fine, these things take time, it will be slow, very slow.

Theo says no. It's fast. Last week she got lost on Barrington and parked in front of the house on Morris where she hasn't lived for fifteen years. She sat there for five hours and missed two work meetings before she called anyone. Gavin cups his friend's hands and Theo gives in to a long silent sob and they are three thirty-year-old men sitting in a dark bar with eyes wet and throats burning, helpless against the gnaw of decay.

Gavin and Zara and Ezra are sitting in bed watching a documentary about Margaret Howe, a British researcher who lived in a place called "The Dolphin House" in the 1960s. Ezra lies on Zara's belly, legs splayed like a frog's, grinding his nose into whatever hand he can reach until the head-scratch continues. The Dolphin House was run by a hippy scientist named John Lilly who performed experiments such as injecting dolphins with LSD. Howe's job was teaching English to a bottlenose named Peter. The research ended with Peter moving to a tiny, dark, half-septic pool in Miami and choosing to simply stop breathing, to descend to the bottom of that toxic, lightless pool as the air seeped out of him. But before that there were the dolphin hand jobs. A vet mentions that dolphins often prefer humans to their own kind and implies that Peter was in love with Howe. Howe herself is strangely forthcoming about the fact that, when his desire got in the way of her research, she satisfied Peter manually.

After the film, Zara tells Gavin about the time she swam with dolphins. Her family went to a resort in Mexico and she spent the days sunbathing and playing ping pong with a boy from Rhode Island whose mouth was a snare of braces.

She and her sister begged until her mother took them on the overpriced excursion and when they got there it deadened something in her. A small pool and a smell like sewage and cheap old fish. Dolphins chirping in that tiny stinking pool and she knew it was ridiculous but nonetheless felt they were asking her personally for help. She'd once seen a *National Geographic* video with dolphins swimming wild off the coast of Florida. Racing fast through the wide and blameless blue and leaping out of the water before darting back inand she didn't know much about dolphins but as she watched them in that pool chattering for food she knew it was wrong. The whole thing was wrong.

Though Gavin wants to, he doesn't say who are we to be the arbiters of animal life.

They lie together in silence for too long and then Zara says, "We're okay, right?" Her eyes pulse like minute oceans, one blue and one green. Gavin says of course and believes it. Believes that they are okay, fundamentally. Believes that this crisis will make them closer, the way collagen thickens a broken bone.

Gavin ushers Ezra out of the room and the dog watches plaintive as the door swings closed. As he pulls Zara in, Gavin finds himself thinking of that lonely dog curled on the far side of the door, listening to the squelch and creak of their union. He wonders whether Zara, too, is thinking of Ezra. But he doesn't ask.

Gavin's task is pulling the meat out of the lobsters, putting the big chunks in the fish tray marked "lob fet" and the small stuff in the one marked "lob rolls." Gavin, who has dreams of starting a vegetarian bistro with Zara and growing their own rosemary and oregano and cucumbers on the patio, is the person the red-faced chef chooses to boil then vivisect these crustaceans. Gavin who is studying cooking at NSCC and works here at minimum wage because of an agreement between the restaurant and the college. Gavin who plans to get his red seal, who has plans to stage in Chicago and Brooklyn. Gavin who has recently mastered garlic-scape pesto, who dreams of tapping his own maples and baptising pistachios in their syrup, who has designed a seven-course meal including onion confit and cayenne mushroom bisque and ending with salted caramel-apple profiteroles. This is the person they elect to drop live animals into boiling water before manually dissecting them, the person who will go home and wash his hands again and again and still be unable to rid his flesh of the chalky aftermath of the bodies he has torn and plucked and mangled.

With each exoskeleton he slices open and snaps off, with each intact tail he eases out of its sheath, with each pea-greensludge of tomalley he spatulas into the fish tray, Gavin thinks about Ezra. Ezra lying inert under general anaesthetic as a faceless surgeon slices open his scrotum, seeking the small slick planets she is paid to extract.

Gavin makes an incision and turns a lobster over to tear the tail off, finds the underside coated with a slick beard of eggs. The green-black beads clinging to that pale red tail and Gavin thinking of the lives these creatures might have had. He remembers reading about a lobster that traveled 273 miles between Maine and Nantucket, knows they often walk vast distances to lay their eggs. But these ones would have lived differently, conceived in hatcheries and grown in a suburb of tanks and filtration systems, of regular testing and men with thick gloves. Gavin thinks of all these dark, alien animals growing strong and fat and reproducing and none of them marching freely through the ocean, none of them hunting by night or hiding their eggs in the swaying deep, none of them birthed amid the dark and flowing greens of rock weed, alaria, or kelp.

Gavin comes to live in thrall of the procedure. His mind a gothic slideshow of veterinarians and gleaming surgical steel. After weeks squinting through screen-blue darkness after Zara goes to bed, he knows the operation so well he thinks he could perform it. He becomes enamoured with the epididymis and the term *vas deferens* derived from the Latin for "vessel" and "carrying-forth." This glandular circuit an escape route for sperm, most of which will be released into hostile terrain and die. The term reminds him of the great, churning tides of the Bay of Fundy. The tide and the sperm, the mind and the moon, all of it always carrying forth and this scientist species wanting to mute that motion, to dam the waterways of life. He writes a suite of poems based on this metaphor but it brings him no closer to a decision.

And the dog ages steadily, the surgery more traumatic by the day.

Two mixed terrier puppies entered their world and Gavin had no precedent for the way they would bend his life, the way his mind would buckle and zing. They called the smaller one Ezra and the bigger one Pound and when Gavin lay down to read both of them would crawl onto his chest and stare at him, the breath gradually slowing in their tiny puppy lungs. They eventually gave Pound to a friend of Zara's and it was just the two of them and Ezra, their one-bedroom flat with the screeching bathroom fan and the warped back door with the glitchy lock transformed into a palace of canine glee.

Gavin had never had dogs as a child and the bond was baffling to him. The trill in his heart when he let Ezra off leash and watched him take off across the grass, front legs barely visible as they scooped and dug into a pinball blur of forward, forward, forward. Gavin was baffled by the joy he took in Ezra's habit of carrying a stick that was far, far too large for him, bouncing it off the calves of anyone who walked near. And he was astounded by his despair, his bottomless torment the day he watched that pup scamper too close to a fat-wheeled Norco, heard the crunch of busted tailbone and the dog's awful pinse of betrayal. A sound Ezra had never made before and how could Gavin not hear it as his own failure, stooping to comfort his puppy and wishing that he himself could have licked that frail bone back together.

And now Gavin has to choose. He has to decide whether or not to wilfully hurt this creature he has done everything possible to protect. He must decide whether or not to extract something vital from this beloved companion's insides, something that could bring him pleasure and excitement and riveting carnal bliss. Gavin must decide whether to permanently maim this cherished friend, whether to flatten Ezra's world.

The shadow was dark and round and when he looked closer he saw it was a mine. A massive underwater mine, the curved and rusted iron slick with a mucous of algae, a gnarled barnacle braille. He thought of Mr. Healy in Social Studies class, talking about the 3,000 unexploded bombs left in the harbour by German U-boats. A chore to remove those explosives and most of them dead by now so the traffic passed through in the hopes that nothing shifted or changed its mind.

Gavin was drifting towards the rust-gnawed mine when Nancy appeared, beckoning him. Nancy flickering in the watery dark and it was only the two of them there in the liquid emptiness where no pollution or creatures or bombs could harm them. He saw her beckon and without a movement of leg or arm, felt himself drifting closer.

Gavin gets up early to walk Ezra around the block and then he makes Zara a burrito fried in handfuls of the garlic he plucked last week from the backyard. She roams naked and fat-eyed into the kitchen, cups him from behind as he whips the guacamole. "Smells gorgeous," she says and he is surprised, as always, that all it takes is the fragrance of bulbs frying in oil to blend this discord of rooms into a home. He says she smells gorgeous and she laughs, filling a mug with the coffee he's just pressed. She sits down at the table, steam rising from her cup, and Ezra nuzzles into her calf. Gavin wonders, briefly, if the dog is stirred by the sight of this naked woman. He wonders this but does not say anything, does not say anything of the sort as he serves breakfast and sits down to eat. They talk about Gavin's work, about his fall courses, about the cherry tomatoes finally ripening in the one patch of full sun. Zara asks about Corinne and Theo, suggests that they have them over for dinner. Gavin says they're doing well and Theo has a gig teaching environmental philosophy at SMU in the fall. He's reached the middle of a spiel about the student-as-customer model before he realizes that he's not telling Zara about Nancy. He's not telling her and he's not going to and what does this mean? Ezra is rising onto his hind legs to sniff at the table scraps and Gavin knows sharply, darkly, that he will not tell Zara about Nancy or Blue Velvet or the early onset. Instead, he sneaks Ezra a peanut and scratches the dog's eager ears and thinks about swelling ventricles, a shrinking hippocampus. He smells Ezra's fetid breath as the dog's tongue licks the sweat from his neck and thinks of the plaque and tangles in Nancy's head, the disease boring her brain like sugar mining a tooth.

There's a bald man Gavin has never seen before at the dog park. He has a little black pug mix and a T-shirt that reads *#alldogsmatter*. When someone asks him what breed his dog is Gavin hears him answer, loudly, "He's a rescue." Gavin stays to the outskirts, talking to Chimichanga's owner and trying not to hear the man lecturing about microchips and puppy mills and shock collars. But the rescue takes an interest in Ezra as he raises his leg to mark the fence and when the smaller dog approaches Ezra yaps at him. The owner scuttles over as the dogs bark and growl. Ezra lunges, teeth bared. Gavin races towards Ezra but he's not quite there when the owner bends to scoop his dog up into his arms, the worst thing he could do.

Ezra goes manic and leaps for the pug mix, who squirms out of his owner's arms and lands on the grass in a rage of growls and bent necks, a fury of teeth and bulging eyes. Turf and fur spin in the air as the dogs tussle and snap and bite, both owners trying to wrangle their snarling pets. Gavin finally grasps Ezra's collar and the bald man yanks his dog back up into his arms and Gavin tries to say sorry but the man is shouting at him.

Gavin hears curses and gibberish and finally makes out "Jesus man, get ahold of your dog!" The adrenaline swells through his neck and chest, his biceps coiling. He knows whatever he says will be brash so he stays silent as the man asks with a quavering voice, "Is your dog even neutered?" It is not a question but an assault. Gavin gets Ezra on leash and as they walk away he hears the man shouting, "How dare you!"

At home he is trembling as he tells Zara the story then announces that he won't be going to that dog park anymore. He can no longer abide the PETA brigade, these people with all the answers. He will take Ezra to Point Pleasant or the Commons and he will simply walk, walk where he and his dog are not cornered in this bastion of norms.

Zara shrugs and says, "Do what you've got to do," turning back to her laptop. He feels it like a foot to the gut. Wishes that just for once she would simply take his side.

Gavin sits down at his desk and starts a poem about doggie pills and doggie condoms. At the end Bob Barker appears on the stage of *The Price is Right*, wagging his liver-spotted fingers at a nation of suburban dream-home gamblers, commanding: "Thy dog shalt not fuck."

Pro: less prone to aggression.
Con: may not reliably reduce aggression.
Pro: dog will be calmer around unspayed females.
Con: almost no unspayed female dogs left in urban dog culture.
Pro: more focused on companion human.
Con: dog will spend two weeks healing with head in cone.
Pro: reduces leg-lifting.
Con: triples risk of obesity.
Pro: reduced likelihood of testicular cancer.
Con: dog will be unable to reproduce.
Pro: dog will be unable to reproduce.
Con: coat may become patchy and haggard.
Con: may lead to hip dysplasia.
Con: ligament rupture.
Con: hypothyroidism.
Con: osteosarcoma.
Con: geriatric cognitive impairment.
Con: risk of death from anaesthetic complications.
Con: risk of death or injury from surgical complications.
Con: wilfully mutilating another living creature.
Con: wilfully mutilating another living creature.
Con: wilfully mutilating another living creature.

Cindy, who'd clearly had a couple of pinots before they got there, has already put her hand on Zara's thigh and winked at Gavin while hissing "this one's a keeper" and now she's talking about cats. They had ordered Thai food because Cindy claims not to know how to cook vegan and now the table around them is a Styrofoam jungle. Gavin tries to ask his mother about her new boyfriend the Via Rail conductor and then tries to ask about her job at Canada Post HQ but she glares over her glasses and keeps on about the feral cats. There are swarms of them in the neighbourhood, she says, fucking and fighting and eating all the songbirds, spreading diseases among the housecats. Cindy looks right at Zara as she rants, one eye drooping and the other fierce with an intimacy not natural between two women who've only met six or seven times. Cindy says one night a feral cat got trapped in her basement and it was spraying and crazed and she had to try to beat it out with a hockey stick but it would not move. So here she was, Cindy, alone in her own house with this cat locked in a room and the window was open but the beast would not vacate. They stayed up all night like that. Cindy tried to sleep but she could feel the cat there, poised and fearful, and in the morning she found it precisely where she'd left it in the corner of the room. She had breakfast and watched it some more and finally realized it must've been desperately hungry so she put some cold chicken by the back door with a saucer of milk and she left the house. Went around the corner to get a coffee. Waited as long as she could. When she came back the cat was gone, the dishes licked spotless.

Cindy smiles smugly and pours herself more wine. Gavin exchanges a look with Zara and asks what the story has to do with feral cats and Cindy says sterilization. We need to sterilize them, of course. A silence thickens in the room and Gavin lets it linger.

Gavin is readying himself to leave when Cindy invites Zara downstairs to see the collection. Zara looks surprised and says of course and so they head down to the basement where Gavin's mother keeps her hoard of children's body parts. They stand among the dust and the suitcases, looking at Gavin's umbilical cord—grey and curled and stiff in its dusty Ziplock womb. The teeth come next. Why would his mother have kept every baby tooth and wisdom tooth and molar Gavin's growing body ever shucked? After the teeth there are jars of hair: Gavin's grade two rat tail, his grade ten Mohawk, his grade twelve surfer curls. As Gavin stands embarrassed in the midst of his personal mausoleum he wonders what would become of Ezra's testes if they were removed. Zara recently told him about rendering and deadstock, about how "livestock management" companies cruise farms collecting horse and goat and cow carcasses, pulping those bodies into the stearic acids and slip agents that become bike tires, shampoo, plastic bags. Now he finds himself wondering if Ezra's gonads will be cycled into kibble, fed back to other dogs in a canine parody of *Soylent Green*.

This is what Gavin is thinking as Cindy unveils her masterpiece—a hand-made cedar box containing Gavin's hospital bracelet alongside newspaper clippings from the electrocution and curled polaroid photos of the burns that permanently marbled his torso and sent purple tentacles flaring up his arms and calves. The burns he's had to have cut and grafted twice since the accident because the scars stay still as his body grows and ages. Seeing those polaroidsGavin feels the burns brighten under his shirt, feels his gut turn tidal as he recalls the inane and drunken choice to climb that tower. Recalls the strange teenage logic that made him believe he could somehow reach Nancy up there. Gavin burns shameful but Zara is calm and sweet as she looks at each photo and newspaper clipping, nodding at Cindy's comments then leaning into Gavin and whispering, "All of this is what you are, and I love all of what you are."

When Gavin was ten he went with Theo and Nancy to their family cottage in Hubbards. Nancy had just broken up with Theo's father and it was just her and the two boys. They spent three mosquito-droning days at a two-bedroom cabin thick with the smell of pine. There were dunes with prickly grasses and a beach strewn with sun-bleached driftwood and ancient, sagging lobster traps. Each night they had bonfires and watched the stars and Gavin learned to love the taste of burnt marshmallows. On the last day Theo got an ear infection and had to stay in bed so Gavin and Nancy went down to the beach without him. Gavin found a dried-out lobster claw and pretended it was his hand as he put his arm around Nancy's shoulder. When she saw that gnarled pincer at her clavicle she laughed and laughed and he felt himself large and noticed. When they went out into the water she watched him swimming and said "no no not like that" and then taught him how to do a proper breaststroke, taught him it was all about timing—the smooth arc of the arms pulling you forward, the legs coiling together as the arms reset. The frog kick and the forward dart of the hands and that moment of skimming effortless across the surface. She explained it, then showed him. He watched her gliding seal-sleek in a black one-piece and then he got it, felt the astonishing ease of it as he shot through the brisk Atlantic on that still and sunny day.

The cabin had an ancient, rusted outdoor shower with a rotting plywood door. Gavin was eager to wash off the salt and sand and so he rushed into that shower thinking Nancy was still down at the beach and found her naked and stooping to pull the sand from her toes. Her breasts dangling freely, dappled by the patches of sun leaking through the slats. They stood there looking at each other like cats crossing paths in an alley. Gavin took no more than a glance at those breasts—curiously pale, nipples like sand dollars.

She did not say a word to Gavin on the drive home, even though Theo was in the back seat still suffering from earache and he was sitting up front. They drove in silence and Gavin stared out the windshield at the road slithering beneath the bright open blue, saw Nancy's breasts in every cloud.

On the walk home Zara says she likes Gavin's mother. Gavin scoffs and asks why and she says how else would Gavin have developed such a dazzling corkscrew mind. He stops her and they hold each other in the middle of the street, a warm wind cloaking them in a swirl of grass and ocean. They make a pact not to talk about Ezra or sterilization so Zara talks about the tidal turbine in the Bay of Fundy. Highest tides in the world so of course they want to squeeze that churning power into dollars. And of course this green energy might not be so green and the lobster fishermen are concerned about the impact to the ecosystem, about the noise pollution diluting the whale song not to mention the plankton being sucked into the 1000-tonne rotors churning the waters of the ancient cove. The cove that bears the world's only fossilized trace of the moment life managed to scuttle out of the ocean and stagger onto land.

He'd been alone in the dark ocean among the lurking mines until Nancy appeared like a beacon. A younger Nancy, a less complicated Nancy, and as he watched her swim astride him he saw her legs melt and flick into a tail. A tail scaled with glimmering greens and blues, a glowing blur streaking the dark water. The water a volatile blackness and he knew it was cold but he also knew he could not feel that cold, felt nothing but Nancy's pulsing proximity. She swam closer still and he was nothing but the thrill of her. He felt himself dancing in her nimbus and he wanted her. A vague want, a desire that did not involve genitals or fluids or climaxes. He felt himself drained of the precision of drives, acquiescing to a novel, blunt euphoria.

They arrive at their apartment and find the back door swinging open. The dog is gone and Gavin is thinking of course. Thinking of fucking course and he and Zara are grabbing the leash and some treats and blasting outside wailing the dog's name into the clammy summer sky. It's almost midnight but some neighbours are out on the porch and they join in and soon the neighbourhood is a clamour of *Ezz-ra*, *Ezz-ra* and they are rounding two corners and coming out onto Gottingen. Gavin thinks they should split up but he doesn't say this because he doesn't want to be alone he just wants this to be not happening. He wants this not ever to happen but it also seems inevitable that their dog, their puppy, is gone. Inevitable that this tender love would swell and swell and burst.

And likewise inevitable that Gavin should round the corner and turn out onto Gottingen and see a dark furry hump in the middle of the road. See the still-wet blood slanting across the yellow line and say Zara's name in a tone that makes her stop and follow his gaze and sprint into the middle of the road through hornbleat and headlights.

Gavin waits for the traffic to pass and walks slowly behind her, knowing already all he needs to know. He hears Zara sobbing as he gets closer but then her sobs become crazed laughter and he sees that the furry hump in the road is a raccoon, still wheezing. Its tiny mouth quivering, paws scrubbing together.

Gavin looks stupidly around for a shovel but then he is back on the sidewalk, calling Ezra's name again, and Zara is with him. They walk down Gottingen and through the square and then turn back, tracing and retracing the grid between Gottingen and Agricola, fattening the night on the name of their dog. Finally they agree to split up and Gavin says he'll go home to notify the SPCA which is no doubt ridiculous but he does not know what else to do. When he gets home he finds the back door still slung open and Ezra cringing in the kitchen, sitting obedient and fearful. Gavin bends down and hugs him, feeling a brilliant and boundless love. More love than he'd known there could be in the world.

Nancy iswordlessly calling him closer as she sways her green and gleaming tail but he can't get near enough to touch her. Something keeps him an arm's length from her face and shoulders and when he reaches up he finds that there is a large cone over his head. A cone that he cannot remove. He looks down to see whether there is a scar between his legs but he cannot see past the cone. She is calling to him, begging him closer, but the cone is between them. Has always been and will always be between them. Eventually she turns away from him and starts to pump her tail. She swims slowly, looking over her shoulder, her hair luffing like seaweed in a current. She is leaving and he is sinking down into the accumulating darkness, watching her shrink into the distance as he drifts into the bottomless below.

Gavin awakes in the gut of night to find the bed empty. He listens to the quiet, locates a ripple through that silence and hears it swirl into murmur. Zara's voice. He thinks of calling her name then thinks no. Instead he rises quietly and leans into the hall, watches her stoop over Ezra, rubbing the sweet spot above his haunch. Gavin hears her cooing and talking a formless gibberish that sometimes settles into "oh yes" or "Ezzy" or "good boy."

And then he sees it, a slick tulip blooming between Ezra's legs. A tube of lipstick winding upwards from a bulb of fur. He knows Zara cannot see that wet and urgent flower as she leans over and rubs his back, and he knows that this canine erection might have nothing to do with her. But he also knows, as he watches this scene of intimacy, that there is something in that small sprout of flesh that he detests. Something that makes him uneasy. And he knows, knows and hates himself for knowing, that for all his talk about hypocrisy and repression and consent, he would be happy if that organ were to disappear.

Zara turns and sees him standing there in the door frame. She does not appear surprised. "I've decided," she announces, still stroking Ezra's neck. "It's up to you." Gavin has to ask her to repeat herself and she says again that it should be up to him, that he cares more than she does and so if he feels like he needs to leave Ezra's genitals intact that's fine with her.

Gavin puts a hand on the door frame. His heart is a fish flapping on a beach. No way out of the choice and no way to make it. "It's on you," she says and the onus slithers down his throat, fattens there. He thinks for the first time in their eleven months living together how easy it would be to leave her. How possible. To leave Zara, leave the lobsters, take Ezra to a cabin in Bridgewater and write poetry, live on beans. The thought is ugly and rank and he tries to dismiss it but it lingers like an eel in his sternum.

Give the animal a mild sedative and inject with general anaesthetic. Place the gas mask on the muzzle or slip a tube down the animal's trachea to administer the isoflurane. The anaesthetic gas will ensure the dog remains unconscious throughout the procedure. Once the animal is fully unconscious, make an incision at the tip of its scrotal sac, taking care not to sever the urethra. Pull one testicle out through the seam in the animal's skin. Trim away the fatty tunica vaginalis, exposing the testicle. Clamp the testicular blood vessels and the vas deferens to ensure blood does not flow upon laceration. Slice the spermatic cord above the clamp, severing the testicle. Discard. Repeat. Suture.

Gavin is walking Ezra on the main path overlooking the Northwest Arm as sunlight flickers down through the spruce. Squirrels scamper after bird feed. A seal chirps in the distance and Ezra bounds through the forest, staying close to Gavin and mostly ignoring the dogs on the main path. This is what

Gavin likes: just walking. No standing in parks talking about groomers and breeders and crate training. What he likes is walking with his companion, the dog off-leash and racing through the forest as Gavin treads the gravel tongue running through it. Ezra returning now and then for a check-in, tongue curling out of his delirious grin. What Gavin likes is watching Ezra tear after squirrels, reaching full speed on the straightaway and then bounding impossibly over stumps and rocks. Watching Ezra stand ankle-deep in the glint of the surf and tilt his head to make eye contact, to share the measureless wealth of his glee.

Gavin is basking in this primal rhythm, the yoked locomotion of human and dog, when they run into her. He doesn't realize it's Nancy until she bends down to pet Ezra.

He is thirteen and stealing her personal sex toy and parading it around the neighbourhood. He is thirteen and unable to forgive himself and climbing an electrical tower and shooting deathbound across the night. He is thirteen and seeking Nancy in each rung, finding her in the brilliant wattage that sends him soaring through the cloudless black. Finding her in the tree that catches him, its leaves lush and soft as velvet. He is recovering in the hospital from six broken bones and third-degree burns across his torso and limbs and feeling all of his pain, all the lifelong scars on his back and thighs as penance. A penance he craves.

Nancy finishes petting Ezra and looks up, looks straight into Gavin's face. He can tell she recognizes him, but distantly. For a moment he inhabits her and sees himself as blur, as echo.

He wants to say hello, wants to tell her it's him, Gavin. Gavin whom she's known for twenty years. Gavin who accosted her and professed his rabid, lifelong desire two years ago at her son's wedding. Gavin who charmed her with a lobster claw and saw her pale breasts swaying in the patchy Hubbards light.

She is gone, loping casually down the path, before he can say any of this.

How could he know, then, that after taking Ezra to a beach strewn with six-pack rings and cigarette butts he would walk down to the parking lot and see Nancy drifting ghastly from car to car, her white hair streaked with a memory of black. That she would turn shrunken and ancient, old as the Sibyl of Cumae. That she would hold a set of car keys in her hands and glide about, pressing the button over and over but hearing no welcoming beep. That when she saw him approaching she would turn to Gavin and, still unable to conjure his name, ask if he had seen her car, a red Toyota, and he would see the exhausted frenzy in her eyes and almost hear the frantic pant of her thoughts. *The car is Red. No. Yellow. The car is red no yellow or was that the last one the car is definitely yellow or red no yellow and where has it gone someone must have taken it, stolen it. The car is a Toyota. A little yellow Toyota Yaris and I bought it yellow for precisely this reason and now I cannot find it in this parking lot. This horrible parking lot and I've been here before been lost here before and why can't somebody help? Of course they can't help because the help I need is not someone asking what kind of car and are you alright but someone crawling into my brain, burrowing through the cavities of my aged and rotting psyche and whispering gentle music, lathering my mind with tea leaves and eucalyptus and mint. The car is red no yellow maybe blue and how I wish I could howl, how I long to wail into the ocean wind and all I want is my car who has taken it someone must have stolen my car. The vehicles like liquid, like gelatine oozing through the lot and none of them mine. A slur of greys and blacks, Nissans and Fords spinning crookedly together in this cackling concrete funhouse and now this boy, this strange familiar awful boy and has he stolen the red no yellow Toyota?*

Gavin makes all this from a twitch of her eye and he says let me help you, maybe you're in the upper lot, let me call your son. Her eyes flit about and she shakes her head in vigorous refusal but when her mouth finally open she is saying yes, saying okay, sure, thank you.

How could Gavin have known that a full third of his lifespan would seem to burn and wither, that his entire life thus far would seem to melt as he phoned his friend Theo, found out that the car was a blue Kia, took Nancy's hand with its colony of liver spots. How could he have known that as she drove out of the parking lot he would glimpse her face through the driver'sside window and wonder once more how someone so lovely could possibly decay. He would realize, then, that he would one day have to tell Zara the whole story. But how could he possibly explain this cosmic beacon, this wounded siren, this disintegrating god?

Gavin would always carry two parallel versions of the experience. He knew what happened and what didn't happen. What didn't happen was he didn't float endlessly underwater, not needing to breathe. What didn't happen was he didn't meet Nancy and watch her sprout a mermaid's tail and beckon him towards a rhapsodic unknown.

What did happen was three kids on a freakishly hot day in early June doing mushrooms and traipsing through Point Pleasant, thinking it was a fun idea to go swimming in the harbour. What did happen was a poor choice. What did happen was Gavin lost Drew and Theo and wound up crawling ashore in Dartmouth and the night got a little colder than expected and he walked alone and soaked in just boxers across the McDonald Bridge. What did happen was he did not shower that night and when he woke up he knew instantly. Even before he looked down and saw the red sores and the slugs of plasma he knew it was bad. Cindy made him eat some cereal and take a shower and she didn't say anything because she didn't need to. She drove with all the windows down to mute the reek of his flesh. The doctor was a kind old grandmother until he said about the harbour. At which point she made him repeat that he'd swam in the harbour and asked what had he been on and as he admitted about the mushrooms he felt as if all the water had fled his body. What did happen, as the matronly doctor explained in arduous detail, was that every miniscule laceration on Gavin's body—every paper cut and bug bite and shin nick from his walk through Point Pleasant—had become infected. What did happen was the doctor took a semi-permanent marker and drew circles around every one of those infected wounds and said if the red reaches this line then come back for antibiotics. What did happen was Gavin spending two plus weeks at school wearing long sleeves every day to try to hide the strange new nipples blooming all over his body and the doctor-drawn circles framing them. What did happen was shame and agony and even less interest than usual from girls and constant ridicule from Drew and Theo.

But what did happen remained much less important to Gavin than what did not happen. What did not happen—Nancy, the mine, the mermaid's tail—was a companion that would always travel with him, a beloved phantasm that would shape and sustain him more than the bland and barren real.

Gavin and Ezra walk home along the waterfront and there are men fishing in the harbour and somehow this has never signified as it does now. Ten or twelve men standing along the wharf and two of them pulling up small wriggling mackerel or cod and the harbour does not reek as it used to. Men out with their sons and daughters fishing and possibly even eating what they fish, which means there is life blooming in the water Gavin knew as an embarrassment of sepsis. There are fish living and thriving and the colour of the water has changed. The water is blue-grey and swaying with seaweed where Gavin remembers a childhood of looking down to see nothing but the spectral orb of a jellyfish, a tampon applicator drifting like an orphaned pinkie.

Gavin walks into their apartment and loves it—loves the clusters of cobwebs and the peeling paint, loves that warped and finicky back door, loves this place that has become a cradle for him and Zara and Ezra. He drops the dog's leash on the floor and holds Zara. Holds her as if his squeezing could weld them into permanence. Ezra scurries about their feet and Gavin delights in this dog and this woman and the things that he now clearly knows. He knows that he has never resented Zara. Knows he has never begrudged this strange-eyed person blending cashew butter in the apartment they share. He squeezes her and tells her he has confused freedom with desire. He has invested far, far too much in a satchel of fluid and hormone. He has seen Nancy lost and confused in a parking lot and she has whispered in her oracle way that what he wants is to take care of others, these others. That she, Zara, is a lovelyconfusing slash of colours and scents and all he wants is to keep discovering her, to brew her French-pressed coarse-grind coffee, to make her mango salad and coconut curry and vegan chocolate torte, to trace letters on the back of her hands as she lilts into sleep, to watch the streaks of white bloom like sun-bleached seaweed in her black, black hair. He tells her that he has agonized over this decision but now he knows it is not a decision, it's a feeling. That there are different ways to care and he can only do it the way that feels honest and real.

He says all this to Zara and she does not need to ask about Ezra because she has always known his decision. She says they will be alright, that things will change and things will stay the same but life is astonishing. She tells him life will churn on and there's no way to know what will happen, let alone control it. She tells him there were palm trees on Antarctica once, tells him this peninsula is just the blunt crown of a weary mountain, a drawling collision of Gondwana, Avolonia, Laurentia. She tells him things will flourish and things will melt. That nothing will be the same but she will protect him. She will hold him against the tidal drone and the vanishing whales and the waters rising to subsume them. Guard him from the acid ocean gnawing the soft sandstone of this peninsula. She vows to keep him safe from the glaciers, melting awake from their long sleep. Safe to listen to the lullaby— chirps and bellows of humpbacks pealing through the oceanic vast. Safe while the restless currents of mind and memory carry forth into the wavering beyond.

ACKNOWLEDGEMENTS

Some of these stories, in earlier forms, have appeared in the following journals and anthologies: *The Puritan*, *The Fiddlehead*, *EVENT*, *enRoute*, *The Dalhousie Review*, *The Antigonish Review*, *Canadian Notes & Queries*, and *Best Canadian Stories 2017*. Thanks very much to the editors and volunteers.

"Enigma" won the 2016 CBC Short Story Prize. "Silicone Giddy" was shortlisted for the 2015 Peter Hinchcliffe Fiction Award. An early version of "Drift" was longlisted for *The Fiddlehead*'s 2017 Short Fiction Prize. Thanks to the readers and judges.

Thanks to: my editor, John Metcalf, for seeing something of value, for pushing me to take it further, and for being a mentor, an advocate, and a friend. My agent, Stephanie Sinclair, for her professionalism, integrity, and enduring support. Dan Wells, Natalie Hamilton, Chris Andrechek, Casey Plett, and everyone at Biblioasis. Aaron Kreuter for careful and generative readings of many of these stories and for ongoing friendship and inspiration. David Layton for helping me turn a tangle of stories into something approaching a book. Helen Walsh and Diaspora Dialogues for providing a vital mentorship community. Daphné Santos-Vieira and everyone involved with the 2016 CBC Short Story Prize. Tyler Willis for being an insightful, rigorous, and creative editor. Old allies Kate Millar, Ian Colford, and Anne Marie Todkill. Joshua Schuster for nourishing me intellectually. Alex Zellner for submerging. Dave Janzen for Sitzpinkling. Tom Cull and Blair Trewartha for farming. Steph Korn for friendship, hospitality, and laughs. The wardroomers: Rohit, Andrei,

Brad. Peninsula dwellers: Tim Sullivan, Stu Hayward, Ross Higgins, Iain Sutherland, Simon Fraser, Jake Thurgood, Mike Dolphin, Rob Fris, Jason Phillips. Diana Samu-Visser and Mike Gyssels for neighbouring. London writer friends Andy Verboom, Kevin Shaw, Madeline Bassnett, Karen Schindler, Kate Lawless, and Kailee Wakeman.

Les Bastien: Isabelle, Richard, Michelle, Daniel, Debbie, Leïla. Rachel Huebert and her family, Jochen and Marie.

My firmament: Ron Huebert and Elizabeth Edwards.

My ocean: Natasha. My garden: Rose.

David Huebert grew up in Halifax, Nova Scotia, and lives in London, Ontario. His stories have appeared in magazines such as *enRoute*, *EVENT*, *The Puritan*, *The Fiddlehead*, and *Canadian Notes & Queries*, and received awards such as the Sheldon Currie Fiction Prize and the CBC Short Story Prize. David is also the winner of *The Walrus'* 2016 Poetry Prize and the author of the poetry collection *We Are No Longer the Smart Kids in Class*.